OBSCURE ORIGIN

ZARA HOFFMAN

ZH
press

To my writer friends:
You inspire me to reach for the stars.

P.S. Mom, family, and family friends: you should <u>skip</u> this one.

There could be shadow galaxies, shadow stars, and even shadow people.

STEPHEN HAWKING

1

VERITY

VERITY WOKE SUDDENLY as a loud rumble vibrated through her room. She closed her eyes again and rolled over. But then flashes of light danced across her eyelids. Guess she wasn't going back to sleep anytime soon. She walked to her window and saw something move at the edge of her field of vision. Verity squinted and saw what looked like a shockwave move through the air: a violent distortion of the air that looked like a heatwave moving with enough power to sway the trees outside. Or like the shockwave preceding the blaze of an atom bomb detonating. It was barely visible in the darkness, but it was there all the same. She couldn't find a clear source, but she had a sinking feeling she knew what it was.

How many times had her father talked to her about the possibility of an invasion? It was the whole reason they were stationed at Groom Lake in the first place. His job was to prepare them for when it did happen.

She never fully believed in the threat, but she couldn't deny what was right in front of her, even if she couldn't fully explain or describe it.

The noise kept getting louder until it was almost deafening

before it completely ceased. It was more than just silence. Despite being firmly on the ground, she felt as if she were trapped in a complete vacuum like an astronaut in space.

And then, as if the impromptu sound barrier had been broken, all the noise rushed in, threatening to shatter her eardrums. The rumble was deeper and louder than before until it sounded like a group of helicopters were all hovering very close. The sound was joined by a piercing series of sustained beeps as the house alarm sounded below. She wasn't just imagining things. There was an intruder in her home.

She could picture the number of STFs—they were basically the same as airmen but as part of her father's special Space Task Force—jumping out of bed to answer the call. But would they arrive in time? None of the houses were further than a five-minute walk and whatever attack was happening was moving too quickly for any type of organized response to be effective, even though training for her father's emergency plan had been in effect for the past year.

She heard a fight break out downstairs and then suddenly her father was shouting her name. "Verity! Code—"

He didn't need to finish with the code's title for her to know what was happening. It was a drill they'd run countless times before in the case of a hostile alien invasion—as had every other house and building on the base. But normally the drill was announced through the base's speakers. And the times that he'd decided to test her personally and merely yelled the code like he just had, his had never sounded so panicked before nor been followed by the sound of a fight that he didn't seem to be winning.

She wanted nothing more than to rush downstairs to help him, but on the off chance that this really *was* just a test, then he'd kick her ass for it. Family or not, he'd always taught her to save herself in the event of an alien attack on the base, so different from what he told his men to do—especially those who had families of their own. Every time she asked him, he either didn't answer or turned it back on her, saying, "You don't think your old man can handle it?"

They both knew the answer.

Despite being older than all of the other active-duty squadron members around, Major General Landau could still hold his own. But this was the first time she'd seen evidence to the contrary. If he was losing so quickly, something was really wrong. She pulled the hair tie off her wrist, combed through her hair with her fingers, and pulled her hair into a tight ponytail. Definitely not the most fashionable one she'd ever styled but that wasn't the point. She didn't need it getting in the way during a fight. Then she grabbed the gun from her bedside table, knelt behind her bed, and aimed it at the door just in time for it to be kicked in by the intruders.

They wore armor suits she'd never seen before. They weren't visibly carrying weapons, nor could she see any holstered or concealed on them, so that was a plus. At least they'd be on a closer playing field. But she couldn't underestimate them. The only way they could've reached her was going through her father. Her racing thoughts ground to a halt. Was he already dead? Or dying with no one to help him?

Her room was too small for them to not quickly notice her, so she used what little element of surprise she had on them and immediately fired a shot dead center at the first's chest with such precision her hard-ass shooting instructor would've been proud. When reprimanding someone, he would yell or whisper. Both could be scary as hell. And she'd always had a hunch that he was harder on her because she wasn't actually in the Air Force but merely doing training because her father ordered her to—and for his men to deal with it.

Her shot may have been perfect, but it bounced off harmlessly. She fired once more with the same effect. Useless, then. She kicked the gun under her bedside table so they couldn't get it and stood, her hands up and guarding her face. If they thought she was going to surrender easily, they had another thing coming.

One moved towards her, vaulting over her bed and reaching to grab her arm faster than she'd ever seen practically any military person move, even the best fighters on the base didn't come close. Her attacker was practically a blur, but she still managed to pull away at the last minute. It was one of the first rules of self-defense: don't let them grab you. It only made things harder for you in the long run. The first rule was to avoid the situation altogether but that obviously wasn't an option now.

She pivoted. The masked enemy moved with her.

He ran at her and threw a punch that she easily dodged. *What the hell was that?* He wouldn't have done anything more than clip her shoulder if she hadn't moved and it hadn't been nearly as fast as he had just gone to grab her. Something was off here.

How could he be so much worse at one thing than another. It wasn't like her learning how to do complicated fight sequences or her dance choreography, which required perfect timing and precision. This was throwing a simple punch. Anyone could do it. Granted, an inexperienced newbie would probably hurt themselves, not just their target, in the process. But still. It was ridiculous for him to be this laughably bad.

She felt the other assailant grab her arm. Maybe the other guy wasn't so stupid after all. If his job had been to distract her, he'd certainly succeeded. Stupid mistake on her part, but it was hard to even see them. Did their armor have the same cloaking technology she'd seen their ship use in the sky? It was as if they were blending into the shadows of her room. A real-life invisibility cloak, only strong enough to deflect bullets at point-blank range. She could barely see the outline of them half the time as they flickered in and out of the shadows, and if she hadn't memorized the room's layout, she'd be really screwed. Given how easily one of them was able to grab her when the other failed.

She could think of a few countries with the stealth capability and could theorize about some that might have comparable defensive gear, but she couldn't even guess which might have both aspects perfected into a single set of body armor. And no country, friend or foe, should've been able to penetrate the base's security so easily as to not trip any alarms. She hadn't even heard shooting outside before they'd fought her dad, which meant they'd invaded completely undetected. They either had someone on the inside or were another level threat they weren't prepared for. Neither option was good.

She twisted around and threw a punch. His partner hadn't been smart enough to grab her other arm when he had the chance. Despite her making perfect contact with her target, it didn't give a satisfying crunch. Definitely weird. She kicked his kneecap in and instead of falling to the ground like she expected him to, he remained steadily on his feet and held her arm. This one was clearly better trained in fighting than his companion. She aimed another punch at him with her free hand, but he ducked under the blow and pushed her into a wrist-lock with surprising ease. If she wanted to, she could bend forward and maybe get enough distance from them to have gravity pull her way from them, but it would also likely dislocate her shoulder or wrist. Or maybe both at the same time.

The men stood behind her on either side and now held her arms out as if she were being crucified. As if that were going to stop her. She bent her left arm and shot her captured elbow upwards, nailing the inexperienced one in the jugular, a sure soft spot even though it was covered. She'd expected her elbow to explode with pain coming up such a hard, bullet-proof material, but it felt the same as when she performed similar moves in fight class—where no pads or protection were allowed. At least there, he was as exposed and vulnerable as her.

His head didn't snap back like she expected, but he grunted, and his grip tightened. A panic reaction, perfect. She nailed him again in the same spot, ignoring the pain it caused to resist his hold on her. His grip slipped, loosening enough for her to break free. She grabbed his shoulders and pulled him down into her rising knee. She spun and use the same arm to land a left hook to the jaw of his buddy. He seemed less fazed, but it still made him pause. She grabbed his arm and flipped him over her shoulder, half surprised that it wasn't any harder than when she practiced the move with some of the STFs during training.

They never went easy on her anymore. Not since she beat their second-best student in that year's combat training class that one time. So, when she—a civilian—bested him, everyone had taken notice.

Her dad had been very proud. And then made the whole class do an extra hour of training that day because none of them should be able to lose to his daughter. It had made her the target of a lot of teasing, but it was all in good fun. And even if some of the new recruits had been genuinely pissed at her, none of them would have dared to blame her for what her father had deemed an inadequacy on their part.

Then the instructor, hard ass that he was, had brought forth Tristan to show off his amazing skills. He wasn't a student anymore, having graduated last year and gotten a step promotion to Technology Sergeant, but he had stuck around to be an instructor. was one of the few people around her age she couldn't win against in a fight. He liked to tease her about it all the time, but given he was such a good friend, she knew it wasn't mean-spirited. Normally, she'd just flip him off and they'd burst out laughing. The other person she had yet to beat was her father's protege Ben. It was during free time that he joined the group.

Everyone else she'd ever fought on base were older instructors, and it was never a "fair" fight with them. Although, the art of fighting wasn't like learning a normal sport. The whole point was learning how to hurt your enemy in any way possible before they could do the same to you.

Verity shot towards the door but was quickly caught again by both of them. What she wouldn't give to learn how they moved so well, though she was pretty sure she'd seen Ben move almost as quickly and Tristan move even faster on some occasions. She had never come close to their speed and agility, but she was clearly out of practice, though to be fair, she hadn't taken self-defense in the past two years.

She should've gone for the window since it was a less guarded exit, but there wasn't any a foolproof way to ensure they wouldn't pull her over the edge of the roof with them if she managed to knock them off the roof. She wasn't nearly as skilled as her favorite animated heroine to guarantee taking it up to the roof would only result in her enemies' demise. But *woulda, coulda, shoulda* had no place in an ongoing fight.

What she was able to do was all muscle memory right now and was very different from the dance and conditioning she did every day. Though both required a backward extension of one leg, an *arabesque* wasn't anywhere near the same as a back kick. They weren't even close when you considered foot positioning, aesthetic, and power. Which was why she was having her ass handed to her by these soldiers' unpolished fighting techniques. Because when you put aside their speed and strength, they were sloppy.

Their punches were wide, and the only thing they did well was grab her—which was as much her fault as their talent. Not that it mattered too much anymore now that they had her trapped more efficiently than the first time. She struggled, but now with both of them holding her tighter than before, gripping her shoulders and pulling her arms back behind her—practically dislocating them—she couldn't shake them off.

Another one came in. He wore much of the same uniform as the others but there was an insignia on his chest. It didn't exactly glow but it reflected light more than the rest of the uniform, making it easier to see. She couldn't get a good look at it, but it resembled a group intersecting geometric shapes. She'd worry about that later. It didn't matter right now. Using the leverage of the ones holding her, she kicked the newcomer with all her might. He fell back a single step and immediately retaliated with a punch to her lip, snapping her head back. She was still swallowing the copper taste when he pointed what looked like a gun at her head. She waited for the shot, but it never came. Instead, he said, "Take her, and let's go."

She glanced up and realized what she had mistaken for a gun was instead a radar reader of some sort. It looked like something out of a science fiction movie, only further confirming that these weren't normal enemy soldiers. Which meant she'd be in a hell of a lot more trouble if they got her outside.

She suddenly went limp, letting her entire body weight take her down. Instead of startling the soldiers into releasing her again, they merely moved with her and pulled her back up before she could completely fall.

They lifted her, her feet no longer touching the ground, and forced her to follow him out of her room, down the stairs, and past her father's prone body. Her eyes started to burn with tears. She tilted her head up slightly before any could fall. She'd be damned before she cried in front of these enemies. And she didn't have the time or luxury to be sad. Survival first. And her dad would remind her to do the same if he were conscious. "Dad—"

"He's not dead yet," the stranger in front of her said. She expected him to ruthlessly murder her father right then but despite the murderous gleam in the stranger's inky black eyes, he didn't make any move to kill him. He kept moving and she was forced outside barefoot, making her wish she had been smart enough to put on shoes before the intruders had reached her. The sweltering heat had made sleeping barefoot a necessity but without any protection, if they decided to stamp on her, her feet would probably be the first to be targeted.

And that's when she saw the spaceship. It didn't look like anything she'd seen in fiction or the projected designs of future space stations. It looked a perfect, shiny sphere resembling the polished aluminum ones that had taken over the internet a few years back. With a lot less visibility, of course, thanks to their camouflaging technology. But she knew what it was all the same. What else could the giant, hovering mass be? When a door and walkway was revealed, there wasn't room for any doubts except who were these "people" and why were they taking her? She was the daughter of a Major General but didn't have an actual position on the base. And there was no way they could know that her father shared a little more with her then what the Pentagon had sanctioned, so there was no reason they should want to come after her. Not that it mattered now, as she was forced to walk up into the unknown and leave behind the only family she had. Assuming she got out of this alive, she'd make them pay for what they'd done to her father, and nothing would get in her way.

2

KNOX

"AND WHAT DO you think of the subjects so far?"

Knox and Dr. Mak'en had been watching the data scans roll in as each person had been brought on board. Almost everyone was accounted for except one. While they had already received the final reading, the subject hadn't yet arrived. He glanced at the door. Should he go down and see what was happening for himself? He forced himself to stay seated. Eiz'm was handling it. Beyond that, and perhaps more importantly, Aerue was overseeing the operation in his absence. Eiz'm had volunteered to lead the ground mission this time, but he wanted someone he could implicitly trust to make sure everything went smoothly.

Dr. Mak'en sighed. "Some are showing very minimal levels of compatibility right now. A more thorough examination would be needed to fully assess their current status and then determine how to best maximize them as a subject. A blood test would be the most efficient—"

"No invasive testing. They cannot know what we are doing."

"Do you honestly believe they're smart enough to figure it out? You know our drawing methods leave no trace. If we did it while they were asleep, they'd never know it." Her voice lifted a bit at the end, clearly hopeful that he would change his mind. "And if they were, they'll certainly notice our injections."

She had a point, but they couldn't. Injections were the fastest way to subdue one of the humans without injuring them. Other methods took time. "I said no." He would if he had to, but he knew there were other alternatives to try first. He changed the topic. "Despite their varying levels, they'll all still receive the same treatment?" Personally, he didn't care per se, but eventually they needed to standardize the procedure for when they eventually scaled up the process. Eighteen people was not nearly enough to satisfy their needs.

"Yes, and no, Your Majesty. Same general method, but varying doses depending on what is necessary. They won't even know it's happening."

"And you're sure they won't be able to tell the difference?" Knox asked, staring at the bowl of food dubiously sent by his chef for Dr. Mak'en's approval. It didn't look appetizing at all, despite being a perfect duplicate of some of the meals he'd seen from his spies on Earth.

"Yes, Your Majesty. Trohm has confirmed it will taste exactly like what they are used to."

His spy on Earth would know better than anyone but he still wished he had actual evidence of a human confirming the undetectability of their special concoction. But if one of the humans tested it before the others and didn't like it, they could tell the others not to trust the food. "Even with the special additions?" he prodded further. If anything gave away that things were not just right, they would no doubt refuse to eat out of pure fear—not even necessarily the determined hunger strikes that peppered human history.

Dr. Mak'en nodded. "Like I said before, they won't notice a thing. It's absolutely undetectable to the human palate. There's no discernible change in consistency either. There is nothing that will raise their suspicions, Your Majesty. I'm sure of it."

"And you'll be able to personalize the meals without an issue?"

"There will be no problems from my end," she answered evenly. "The chefs simply need to thoroughly mix every meal in case a human decides at any point to not finish. If they're not fully integrated with each other, then the dosage will be lopsided. Most importantly, as long as the guards don't mess up the assigned meals, everything will be fine."

"What happens if—?"

She gave him a look bordering on disrespect, but more so personal affront that he would doubt her.

He couldn't blame her. They'd been tinkering with the formula for centuries now, updating it every so often to stay aligned with humanity's evolving culinary skills. For him to still be asking questions must be annoying, not that she would ever say so.

"You briefly mentioned it, but what happens if one of them doesn't finish eating?"

"It shouldn't be a problem. The food should activate the proper receptors in their brains that will make them eat until completion, but if that were to be the case, we could always calculate how much of the dose they did not take—only if it's been mixed correctly like I stated earlier—and then supplement it through other administration methods. Your guards know how to inject them safely, correct?"

He nodded. It wasn't a perfect solution given they could talk to each other after their interrogations, but they would also likely be disoriented and potentially experiencing some light memory loss as side effects from the truth serum. They had reconstructed his grandfather's formula that was used eons ago during the crusade against the Vrulxol and Lielneh. If it had worked on those mountainous brutes and wily enemies, and even the traitors among their own kind, it would easily work on the humans.

A low beep reverberated through the air, signaling the arrival of a newcomer a mere moment before the wall opened to reveal a guard on the other side. He stepped into the lab. "Excuse me, Your Majesty."

Knox turned to the man who had interrupted his conversation. "What is it?"

"The last one has arrived. She was more difficult to obtain than the others."

That was unexpected. She wasn't the only one taken from the last location, and all the others had been brought on in a timely manner. When he'd sanctioned the raids, he hadn't thought it would take them so long. Their first stop had been simple, but he should've known that a site that was kept secret from most of humanity filled with military personnel would put up more of a fight. But given they only had a few marks they still should have been well underway back through the atmosphere before any human could sound an alarm. Snatching people in the middle of the night was bound to draw some attention, but theoretically it would be delayed and too late for the humans to do anything about it. Them finding out so soon wasn't ideal. Luckily, they hadn't needed to kill anyone.

"Where is she?"

"In the throne room, Your Majesty."

"Have Aerue meet me there."

The man nodded and disappeared.

Knox glanced at the biological data and projections one last time and suppressed a yawn. He'd been up for almost a full human day now, going over all the final preparations with the guards, chef, and now Dr. Mak'en, so it was no wonder he was growing tired. He wasn't exactly well-rested now, but the excitement of seeing the final subject was enough to keep the exhaustion at bay.

Knox stood and addressed the good doctor. "Thank you. I'll let you get back to work, but please also get some rest."

"Of course, Your Majesty."

He nodded and took his leave. As he walked down the corridor, he saw guards stationed at each room containing a human. They all acknowledged him with a bow as he passed, and he returned each with a nod.

When he entered the throne room, Aerue was already waiting for him, as was the last and newest guest to his ship. He glanced at the three men holding her down. Were they really necessary? She was just a young woman in sleeping clothes, after all. All the same, two of his soldiers each held an arm while Eiz'm had one hand on her neck and the other tightly gripped her blonde ponytail.

It would take nothing for Eiz'm to snap her neck. It would be easy for all of them to do so, but to use this threat to keep her under control was excessive. At least he couldn't see any bruises forming on her skin underneath his fingers. But she had a bleeding lip. His eyes narrowed. "I thought I said you weren't to inflict any harm."

"We had to," one of the soldiers started. "She was waiting for us when we reached her." He was speaking very quickly and, in his panic, had forgotten to address him correctly, but Knox wasn't about to cut him off. He wanted to hear how this woman had reacted to their intrusion.

"She ambushed us with a gun and fought back," the other chimed in. "She—"

"When I walked in," Eiz'm interrupted, "they were only just containing her." The disdain in his tone was unmistakable, but Knox was impressed.

He glanced at her again and found her staring at him in disbelief. When their gazes connected, her eyes widened briefly before she dropped her gaze to the ground. It was a surprisingly meek gesture compared to what his incompetent soldiers had just said.

"I had to subdue her to get a reading," Eiz'm finished.

"You still disobeyed an order, Eiz'm," he said, causing the man to frown. Calling him out in front of those with lesser rank wasn't ideal, but it needed to be said. Such an infraction needed to be addressed immediately, not left to fester into something worse. They'd had issues before, but Eiz'm had never directly disobeyed before. He hoped it wasn't the start of a new habit. Now that they were ready to interact with Earth, they needed to be a united front.

"You can all go," he said, dismissing them. He didn't need them making the situation more tense. The young soldiers were too anxious, and Knox couldn't deal with Eiz'm for more than a few short doses at a time. And if things got out of hand, Aerue was there to get things back under control.

Eiz'm bowed and backed away then turned and walked out the door. The others departed too but kept their front to him the whole time—as it should be—leaving the woman standing alone with him and Aerue in the room. Her eyes were alert and wary.

"I apologize for how my men treated you. I'm—"

He didn't get to finish before she was lunging at him. He took a step back the same time Aerue intervened, knocking her off balance. Instead of falling to the ground, she barely missed a beat and landed gracefully before connecting two hits to his general and best friend's jaw. It didn't do much harm, but it was still an impressive feat for a human to accomplish. Her victory was short lived as his friend quickly restrained her from behind. He watched her struggle for a few more moments before she realized it was futile. Her baleful glare darkened her beautiful hazel eyes and targeted him with so much intensity that he would've died if looks could kill. He suppressed a smile. This one promised to be a lot of fun, though he also wondered what it would be like to be on the receiving end of a friendly word from her.

She was smart, this one. This whole time, she had been studying him, not staring at him in stupefied wonder like he'd previously assumed. It was a good plan on her part. And it might have worked if the young soldiers were still in charge of holding her, but Aerue was the best of the best. And if by some miracle she had gotten through his best friend, Knox could still defend himself from a human just fine.

Trohm had already said she was special, and as a friend of hers, he was no doubt often saw a happier side of her. He had said that her father had trained her well, but even with that upper hand on some of the other subjects, she still had never managed to beat him in a fight.

Which only made it clearer that the soldiers sent to get her had been vastly underprepared. They had been too new and untrained to go on the mission, but he hadn't been the one to select them. A mistake he wouldn't make again. He'd have to talk about Eiz'm about that later, too. And he would probably have to personally talk to the young soldiers. Picking newbies was completely illogical based on Trohm's reports on her.

Trohm had volunteered to personally get her, but Knox had vetoed it immediately. If she were to recognize him, he didn't doubt that she would use that knowledge to somehow undermine the greater mission. At the very least, he'd have to find a way to silence her from causing a panic among the others. No one could know that he'd had a few undercover agents on Earth before their arrival tonight. It was still bad enough anyone knew about their appearance.

It was already risky enough to have Trohm still posing as his human persona alongside the other captured subjects. It might have been better for this young woman and the men from their location were kept under the mistaken impression that he was merely left behind on Earth with everyone else. He would still be able to observe humanity and report back rather than being confined to the people he already knew very well. Any information he had had been passed through over the years, and anything else could have been as easily transmitted. Knox sighed. There was nothing that could be done about it now.

Before he could speak again, she shot off a question. "Where am I? I wasn't exactly given a tour when I was brought onto this giant, chrome donut."

He chuckled at her description. He supposed it appeared that way, but in reality, the structure was a full disk. Humans simply couldn't see doors leading to the interior rooms, so it made sense that she thought it was a circular corridor and nothing else. For that matter, they couldn't see any of the doors as the edges were imperceptible to the human eye. "My ship."

It had been his father's, who had designed it with his father. It had led their invasion of the other planets in their solar system. When Knox was younger, his dad had taught him all the secret passages and how to drive it. Even though they were royalty, his father had insisted he grow up to be self-sufficient in the event that one day, they lost it all the same way the once invincible Vrulxol and Lielneh had.

She raised an eyebrow at him as if to rebuke him for his brief answer. "You're going to have to be a bit more specific or I'll be forced to believe that this is a crazy, lucid stress dream."

This time, he did smile. She was clearly fishing for information. None of the others had been this forward. Then again, most were barely functioning, suffering from shock to varying degrees. Well, except the man who came before her. Though surveillance had shown that he had been belligerent, even he lacked the fire blazing in this woman's hazel eyes. He had fought back out of necessity and in self-defense. She, on the other hand, was doing it for more than just instinct. There was something slightly feral in the way she had launched herself at him. It was clearly deep and emotional with her, even if it were only hatred rather than fighting for a cause that fueled her punches. It certainly wasn't fear.

The idea of seeing her afraid didn't sit right. He pushed the image away and took a slow step forward, ignoring Aerue's warning look. He watched her face and saw her eyes glance down to see where he landed. No doubt assessing her options. But she and Aerue were both entertaining unrealistic scenarios. Regardless of her fighting abilities, she was still a human. He was safe from any death she planned for him.

It was already difficult for his kind to kill one another. The contingent that had betrayed his grandfather to their enemies had all been eradicated, but it had taken time to slip under their defenses and eliminate them. Even while asleep, Eochronian senses were attuned enough for them to wake in an instant with battle-ready accuracy. There was no way a human could successfully breach one of his kind's defenses.

A part of him wished Aerue would go away and let her have another go at him. Would she change her approach after the first time or was she tactically intelligent enough to adapt? He should have had his engineers equip the grab teams with recording devices in their armor. For now, he'd have to be satisfied with Eiz'm and Trohm's reports. Perhaps one day he'd be able to see her fight. But he wouldn't really fight back. Because just as he was safe from her, she was also safe from harm from him.

For now, though, he'd entertain himself with this woman who showed no signs of giving in easily and see what information he could get from her.

3

VERITY

VERITY SCANNED THE LARGE ROOM, her eyes landing on a metal throne at the far end of the room. It was incredibly ornate with different pieces branching off and coming together as a whole as if synthesized from liquid metal, so different from the corridors she'd walked through on her way here and appeared to be emerging from the very floor it stood on. And it was huge. Much taller than any she'd ever seen in a history book. And some royalty went nuts when it came to designing their thrones so for this one to be even grander was saying a lot. It reminded her a little of the one in the last film of the famous space opera series, only this one was much more polished and shinier and that one had been made out of rough rocks. Both were still more comfortable than the much smaller but equally famous throne of a fantasy series.

At least this throne looked moderately comfortable, or, as comfortable as it could get without any cushions. She wondered who sat there. Probably this guy's father since he had the ability to dismiss the soldiers but was too young to be in charge himself. Besides, if he was the top of the power structure, he seemed like the type of person who wouldn't let anyone forget it. And yet the guy who'd knocked her out—Eiz'm—had clearly disobeyed him. And what type of leader couldn't keep his people in line? A bad one.

She focused back on him, meeting his gaze. He'd taken a step closer once Eiz'm and the goons had left, but there was still enough space between them to protect him from her. And, as much as she hated to admit it, probably her from him. He might have a guard, but he had been way too relaxed and disinterested when she'd gone after him. But the intensity of his stare seemed to obliterate the distance between them and made her feel more exposed than she ever had before in her life. And that included a very awkward first time during a drunken hookup with Tristan that they had vowed to never share with anyone. She shuddered internally at the memory. At least their friendship had stayed intact. If anything, the shared secret brought them even closer.

Even if the man in front of her wasn't the one ultimately calling the shots, he clearly knew why she was abducted. And the others whom she'd seen lined up and afraid. She'd recognized a few of the faces, but most were likely civilians. She could spot a military man from a mile away based on how he stood. And the strangers most definitely did not fit that criterion. Some Aeronautical Space Exploration scientists who had been visiting the past week were also present. Then there was Tristan and Ben who had been the only ones to meet her searching gaze as she passed by. Neither had seemed as terrified as the others, but their bravery and unfazed expressions were unsurprising. They were trained to stay calm under all sorts of situations. She expected nothing less from them. They might be STFs, but they were as serious as they came when the situation called for it. Had they tried to fight them, too, and failed? Neither of them was bleeding or sporting serious injuries like her father, so maybe they had gone more peacefully and were simply biding time?

Before she could even finish the thought, four soldiers marched up to the line and started taking people away. Tristan was one of them. He glanced back at her and gave her a reassuring smile but it did nothing to unknot the tightness in her stomach.

Her lip was still sore and swollen from when Eiz'm had hit her. She wanted to suck her bottom lip to alleviate the pain but there was no way she would show these bastards a sign of weakness. Maybe she should've held back until she could analyze them more. Too late to change the past, but she was flexible and was fine with changing her approach.

Besides, this guy seemed more restrained than the ones who'd stormed into her home. Maybe he was a talk first, fight second type. If he could fight at all. He'd retreated when she'd gone for him and his bodyguard had intercepted her. Her arms were still held above her head and starting to tingle. She must've given some hint of her discomfort because the mystery man made a motion and she was released. Only for her wrists to be cuffed behind her back with what felt like pure electricity and magnetism instead of metal. She tested their strength and felt like she was trying to pull apart neodymium rare earth magnets. Well, that was new. Out of the corner of her eye, she saw her jailer stand at her side, holding something in his hand that looked like an electrical whip connected to her cuffs. He might not be personally immobilizing her anymore, but she was still stuck under his control. For now.

"Like I tried to say before you interrupted me, I'm sorry how my men treated you." He sounded more amused than angry, but the words were too similar to so many villainous quips in books and movies that she still felt like the poor mouse in their cat-and-mouse game. "It's nice to meet you Verity," he finished.

She couldn't help but flinch as if she'd been shocked by electricity. Her cuffs hadn't actually done it, but she felt it all the same. *He knew her name?* "Only my friends call me that."

He raised a sculpted eyebrow. "Am I not a friend?"

She started to turn around, but his guard didn't let her. But the guy must have given a signal because he loosened his grip on her and she rotated to show her shackled wrists and spoke over her shoulder. "I don't know how things work between you and your friends, but friends don't usually chain each other up."

"You're right. I normally wait for them to ask first."

Holy, fuck. Was he admitting to being kinky? And why did that excite her? Sure, he was gorgeous. He wore a tightly tailored shirt and dress pants. They were both black and weren't anything special on their own or even as a pair, but on his body, they looked magnificent. But he was also responsible for her being abducted from her home. That's what mattered more than anything and she couldn't lose sight of it. She wasn't about to be another statistic in Stockholm syndrome sufferers. Although she'd be the first case of a human/alien interaction.

He didn't say anything to follow up, seemingly waiting for her to talk, but she couldn't think of a thing to say. And not because she didn't have anything nice to say, but because her stupid mind was still in the gutter. She mentally shook herself and forced herself to move on. She turned her head and took the opportunity to see the guard who had prevented her from murdering the man in front of her. He'd moved so quickly earlier that she hadn't had time to register any physical characteristics aside from him being larger than any of the soldiers who'd captured her, including Eiz'm. Besides, she needed a break from the smug bastard. Staring at him too long was like looking at the sun—beautifully tempting and an incredibly stupid thing to do.

This guard wore a scowl and had the same insignia on his clothes, but the color scheme was completely different from the all black ensemble Eiz'm had worn. His top had a small, rounded collar about an inch or two thick, not unlike a traditional Chinese qipao, his pants were a matching charcoal. and the symbol was silver, reflecting light that had no apparent source. The planets and stars outside the giant windows weren't enough and she hadn't seen anything in the room or ceiling that could be illuminating the room.

She could feel the other man's eyes on her and faced him again. She'd been avoiding him long enough. And he still hadn't told her where or what his ship was, but maybe he'd respond better to a more general question. "Why am I here?" Though, given his caginess so far, she didn't expect an answer.

"Tell me, what do you know about aliens?"

Was he serious? "They're not real." The lie came easily. The number of times her college friends had asked about extraterrestrials once they learned her father was in the Air Force was ridiculous. And that was without her telling them that she had grown up at Homey Airport—or Area 51, as the media and conspiracy theorists had dubbed it.

"And yet you don't seem fazed about being brought to what you humans call a—UFO—is it?"

She didn't even blink. After hearing countless conspiracy theories at college once her fellow students inevitably learned where she lived, it was easy to not react. Professors always shut down the conversations pretty quickly during class time, probably because the government—or, at the very least, her father—had threatened them on the grounds of national security, but that didn't stop them from peppering her with questions on breaks. "Those don't exist, either." That was the truth, at least. There hadn't been a real *unidentified* flying object spotted in America since the 1940's. Even though they hadn't had a peaceful extraterrestrial encounter or seen aliens up close in their spaceship, like a certain famous 80's film, they had recorded the event with a high enough resolution to remove any doubt as to what had flown through the sky. But that was one of the most locked down secrets of the base. And any videos that had supposedly been released were completely bogus.

He held her gaze, his eyes narrowing in skepticism and concentration as if he were trying to read her mind. When she didn't forfeit the staring match, he looked away and made a humming sound in the back of his throat. It was better than the smirk he'd worn a few times since meeting her, which had only made her want to slap him more, but this made the hairs on her neck raise. What the hell was that? Why could she feel that sound vibrate through her? She must be losing it. It was the middle of the night, after all. She wasn't trained like the squadron members on base to be able to wake and move at a moment's notice. Maybe she should've taken her father up on that opportunity. As it was, she was damn proud of how well she was functioning. And she knew she was handling it much better than the civvies who had also been taken.

The collection of captives still confused her. Aliens had never been documented to take such a large group, much less one spanning different walks of life, at once. Then, again, they hadn't exactly perfected translating ancient texts and glyphs so maybe there was a historical precedent unknown even to the most knowledgeable on the subject in modern day.

She still had no answers, and that was starting to piss her off. And that was on top of her sleep deprivation which already made her into a grumpy monster that everyone on base knew to steer clear of until she'd had her first hit of caffeine. "So, you're telling me that I'm on a spaceship and you're... an alien?"

She made her tone one of disbelief, and it honestly wasn't that much a stretch. Top Secret research aside, she—nor anyone at Area 51 or probably even at ASE—could have expected such an abrupt and boldly antagonistic appearance of extraterrestrial life. It's not like they'd done anything to offend them. Unless the people responsible for sending messages to space through Voyager I had made a terrible mistake.

He took a step forward, and she retreated a step like a coward, bumping into the guard at her back. He didn't even move. It was like hitting a brick wall the same way it had been hitting him. But for a body to be that strong made more sense than for a face to be as hard as titanium.

She felt as much as saw the amusement emanating from the mystery man's features as he silently watched her mental gymnastics. The stupid smirk was back. "Is that so hard to believe?"

"Yes."

Looking at him, he looked as human as any other she'd ever seen. Except for the eyes. They were violet with hints of lapis blue and flecks of white mixed in. They looked like miniature galaxies.

It wasn't evolutionarily impossible for two groups to evolve separately into the same result, but if these *people*, for lack of a better term, really were aliens, the chances of that were literally astronomical. You had to account for the right star and planetary composition, atmosphere and environment, and so many other variables. And they happened to look *just* like humans? Doubtful. But shapeshifting so completely wasn't a realistic alternative either. At least, it wasn't on Earth. Did that mean he was telling the truth? But he had no reason to tell her the truth either. She couldn't take anything he said at face value.

"Your species has spent years trying to find other intelligent life in the universe, and when you finally are confronted with it, you all turn into skeptics—even the ones who believed the hardest when no one else did. It's quite a fascinating phenomenon with you lot. You can't seem to unite over anything, and yet you also haven't completely turned on each other."

The people who died in every war ever, especially the World Wars, would probably beg to differ. Though if humans had killed each other to the point of extinction with the nuclear weapon stockpiles every country denied having, it would be much easier for aliens, like this man claimed to be, to take over the Earth. There would be no one to fight them off, though one couldn't rule out the possibility of science fiction proving to be right yet again and have some mutation effect on remaining life so they could become sentient. The genre had already predicted so many technological advances years before they came to fruition. But that was all irrelevant because humans were still around and at least the ones on the base at home were likely gearing up for war. She forced her tone to stay light. "How are you speaking English?"

He shrugged. "It's not that difficult."

"It is to every speaker of any other language on Earth." Not that she could blame them. English was a crazy hodgepodge of languages that threw out the existing grammar to create its own meandering and inefficient version with a stupid amount of exceptions to every rule.

"Understandable since your kind is very focused on the differences that exist between you."

"I'm sure it makes your job a lot easier."

He smiled the way a predator did right before going in for the kill. "How so?"

"You're clearly here to either enslave us all or to add *homo sapiens* to Earth's extinct species list. If we remain divided, it's easier for you to divide and conquer us. Maybe you plan to wipe out all of Earth's life. Did I miss any other options?"

He shook his head, but it wasn't in the way someone did to say *no*. More like an amused disbelief. Ultimately, it was another non-answer. "You certainly have a wild imagination."

The guard holding her snorted and she wanted to break his nose with the back of her head like she'd tried to do with the soldiers in her room, but if it hadn't worked with them, she doubted it would work now on him. But she hated that these aliens were laughing at her. She knew that she wasn't exactly terrifying, but their condescending teasing was just a dick move that added salt to the wound of being kidnapped.

"If you're not going to reciprocate," her college writing professor would be so happy she used such a fancy word if he could hear her now, "then can I go to sleep? Or are you going to torture me first? I guess my alien movie knowledge won't help me here."

Though if he told her they were mostly accurate, she might actually believe him. Everything that had happened tonight was just proving every alien conspiracy theorist on the planet right. Though, like this stranger had said, she doubted many of them would actually believe it if they met any of these aliens. Maybe the ASE scientists they'd taken were less surprised. After all, they studied space all the time for a living. But there was no reason for her to know the probability of any of this happening so the disbelief hadn't totally worn off yet. She was only human, after all. But right now, that was clearly a disadvantage.

When he yet again didn't answer, she asked, "Well?"

4

KNOX

WHERE DID this girl's unwavering confidence come from? He wasn't convinced he'd be bravely challenging his captor if he were in her position, but here she was undaunted by the reality of her situation as she continued spouting audacious speculations about his motivations for taking her and the others from Earth.

He couldn't remember the last time he'd had this much fun talking to someone. Sure, Aerue gave him shit all the time, and Arfilmea had fun needling him, but it wasn't the same. They teased him because they were his friends but when it came to serious matters, he knew they'd defer to him. Not out of fear, but merely because they had to because he was ultimately their king and they were his subjects. And though Verity was even further under his command than them, she showed no signs of acknowledging or caring about that fact. It seemed nothing would prevent whatever thoughts popped into her head from coming out of her mouth.

If the trend continued, it might be a lot easier to get information from her than the human Captain they'd captured before her. He'd been taken right to interrogation with one of his more experienced soldiers while Eiz'm and Aerue had been busy with the young woman before him.

Then again, her forthrightness now might not translate into opening up about herself or her world. Right now, she was mostly alternating between hurling insults and questions at him. It was easy to see the quick-witted intelligence in her hazel eyes as she responded to him quickly and easily, as if it were as simple as breathing.

He hadn't humored many of her questions with answers because as entertaining as she was, he wasn't about to show his hand. She was a human and therefore a hostile. For now, at least. But that didn't mean he couldn't indulge her wild conjectures a little bit. "I wouldn't go by humanity's imagination to determine what alien life is like, no. But imagination and ingenuity are what got you so far as a civilization and into space, so there's something to be said for it. After all, we're only here because you reached out to us." It wasn't the full truth because the timing was very different from what she was thinking, but at the very least, it wasn't a lie like the ones she'd been spouting throughout their conversation.

He wondered if she suspected he knew she was lying. She seemed too intelligent to be unaware of the fact, but she hadn't brought it up. If on the off chance she didn't know he'd seen through her, he'd let her live comfortably in that false sense of security for a bit longer. If she knew she was beaten, she might change her attitude, and he didn't want that to happen just yet, if at all. Even though Trohm had shared many stories where she stood up for herself, he also knew that when her father or other military officials were around, she tended to reign herself in. He rather enjoyed this spitfire version of her and didn't want it disappearing if his rank came into play. Luckily, no one had addressed him as the king in front of her.

"When?" The word was said with such force it was more a demand than a question.

"I believe you call it 1980 AD," when the first of two missions of the same name left the Earth's solar system. Quite an advanced achievement for what was otherwise a slowly-progressing space program compared to the one spearheaded by his father and grandfather. They had already been traveling through different galaxies by the time he was only 3 millenniums old.

Understanding quickly dawned on her features. The change was so fast, he would bet she had been waiting for him to confirm a hunch rather than asking out of complete ignorance.

It was the first time humanity had reached out to them but it wasn't the first time his kind had visited Earth. That went much further back. He'd personally never gone to the surface of the planet, but some of his soldiers had. Some, like Trohm, had been there for a long time, living through the centuries and appearing to not age to the humans around them. After their first arrival centuries ago, they'd been mistaken as what her species called gods multiple times before modernity labeled them aliens. He wasn't sure which he liked better. In the interim between gods and aliens, humans had called them immortals because no human lived as long as an Eochron and then vampires because *one* of them had been caught tasting a human's blood out of curiosity. He'd been executed quickly after, but the damage had been done and the myth was still alive and well—just as hard to kill as the fictional creature.

Though they'd done little to actively help humanity, they still gave them a lot of credit for their incredible feats when they were worshipped as gods. For example, popular conspiracies claimed aliens built the pyramids, but they had had no hand in the actual construction of them, neither giving direct aid or technology for the slaves of ancient Egypt to achieve the miracles of their construction given their primitive tools. Nor were they responsible for any of the other wonders of the world, as humans had dubbed a host of grand structural achievements.

"Did we insult you?"

Her question lacked any edge or sarcasm and only conveyed a genuine curiosity. He wasn't expecting that. "No," he answered honestly. "Why would you ask that?"

"Oh, I don't know. The kidnapping thing isn't exactly a gesture of peace between two species." Her fire had returned and she appeared to be on a roll. "In fact, we call it *declaring war*, so if your intention was to return what we assumed was a friendly invitation, you missed the mark by a few lightyears."

He smiled. "No, you didn't offend us in your messages," he reiterated. And he knew all about what constituted a declaration of war on Earth from Trohm but he had specifically planned the abductions to happen when they would be asleep and unprepared for an invasion. Certain cities on their planet had the reputation for never sleeping but this wasn't one of them. He'd underestimated them. A mistake he would not make again. Especially not with this girl. "They were very cordial."

"Then you could've landed in a corn field, made some farmer very happy and famous, and then contacted the world leaders for a meeting. Or even gone for peaceful spectacle of broadcasting yourselves from space. So, why all the hostility?"

"Am I being hostile?" Didn't hostility require someone to be more actively antagonistic. He rather thought he was being reserved and polite.

She tipped her head up, looking at the ceiling as if searching for something. "Well, maybe not you, personally, but breaking and entering into a government facility to abduct people is pretty hostile. Assassination and murder would be worse, but still—" She brought her gaze back down and pinned him with an accusatory stare. She waited for an answer he couldn't give.

"I understand." And he'd considered this very problem when deciding whether to publicly introduce themselves or to secretly verify and further observe the subjects in their natural habitats. He changed the topic. "Tell me about what it's like to live in *Area 51*, as you call it."

"First of all, we already established that's a myth." She was clearly sticking with her lie. "Second, I don't have to share anything with you."

Not yet, but she would.

"Then tell me about your friends."

She sighed.

While he waited for an answer, he gave her a once over and was pleased. He'd been too preoccupied with reprimanding the ones who'd brought her in and Eiz'm that he hadn't been able to fully appreciate her beauty before. The tight tank top didn't leave much too much to the imagination, and made it very clear she wasn't wearing any undergarments. The pants, though not form-fitting, clung to her shapely hips. Even in the sleeping clothes she hadn't had time to change out of, he could see her petite body had enticing curves he'd love to explore. He doubted she'd let that happen any time soon, but she wasn't ready for him, anyway. He could be patient.

"What part of me refusing to talk is confusing you? You can ask me as many questions as you want, but I won't answer."

"Didn't you already complain that's what I was doing? I'm simply accommodating your request to be more communicative, even more so than you did."

"Giving vaguer and shorter answers than me isn't accommodating at all. Are you sure you know English as well as you claim to?"

He smiled. "I believe you asked me to reciprocate. I'm doing just that by giving you the same amount of courtesy I received. I'm sorry if you wanted more, but you'll have to give it first if you want to receive."

Her jaw clenched. "This is pointless. I don't care what you do to me, I'm not going to tell you anything."

He wasn't so sure, though he could see he wouldn't get any farther in the conversation right now. He took the leash from his friend and jerked his chin towards the door. "Aerue, get three of the senior guards to escort her to her room."

Her eyes went to where he now held her chains, then lifted to meet his. "You don't really think I need three guards, do you?" Her voice had gotten softer and higher, a show of meekness, but he knew better. "I'm only one woman and your species is clearly superior to humans in both strength and speed, so we both know there's nothing I can do." She didn't continue, but he could practically see her adding a silent, *that I haven't already tried.*

"I think you're underestimating yourself. I know I did at first." He took another step closer, forcing her to tilt her head up to maintain eye contact with him, reminding him again of how comparatively small she was to him. To any of his kind, for that matter. He leaned down, bringing their faces even closer. He suppressed a smile when he saw her eyes dilate. "Rest assured," he murmured, "I won't make that mistake again."

He straightened and took a step back, enjoying the way she remained stunned for a moment before snapping out of it.

Her humble facade fell away, and she shrugged then smiled at him, apparently back in her element. "I guess I should be flattered you think I'm such a threat. I'm sure my dad would be proud." Her tone turned serious. "Assuming he stayed alive long enough to be found." Her death glare promised revenge against anyone responsible for harming her family—including him, though he'd like to see her try.

The guards arrived and stood silently at the door, waiting for his command. He handed one of them the leash. "See that she gets to her room without causing any trouble." The man nodded, and Knox watched as they took her away, one on each side of her and one in front. She'd have a hell of a time escaping them even if her hands weren't tied. And right now, she appeared too exhausted to try anything. He hoped she wasn't putting on an act to lure his men into a false sense of security. Though they were much more prepared than the ones she'd come up against in her home, he didn't need her causing another incident tonight. He intended to treat the subjects well, and if she insisted on regularly attacking his people, he'd have to do something about it or risk being seen as putting a human above his kind.

"I'll see you tomorrow," he called out after her, his voice ringing in the almost empty throne room.

She glanced over her shoulder and spoke through the very small gap between the two guards flanking her. "I'll be waiting with bated breath," she replied with exaggerated anticipation.

He smiled at her dramatic flair. He knew she was being insincere but he was very much looking forward to their rematch. "Have a good night and sleep well, Verity."

She didn't deign his last comment with a response, instead turning her head with enough speed that her ponytail whipped one of the guard's cheeks, but that didn't wipe the smile off his face. His plan was progressing nicely and if things kept going just as or even more smoothly, he'd be able to spend a lot more time with this spitfire.

He turned to see Aerue watching him with a frown.

"What?" he asked, already anticipating the answer. He didn't have much else in the way of entertainment, being surrounded by the same obsequious people day after day, although that had clearly changed with Verity's arrival.

He watched his friend's features as pensiveness give way to realization then annoyance before finally settling on disapproval. His friend shook his head. "You're interested in her."

Knox turned back to the door, wishing he could see her reaction to her living quarters in person. He'd have to settle for seeing it recorded later. Right now, he was falling further into sleep's temptation and if he didn't get into bed soon, his friend would have to carry him like when he was younger and more reckless—partying too hard and too late into the night to be responsible on his own. "Of course I am. Did you see her? She wasn't afraid of any of us—"

"That's not a virtue. She doesn't know any better—"

"Besides," Knox continued, "she's a subject, and therefore warrants my interest. The only female one, too. Why is that?"

"Don't let her mess with your head," his friend warned, ignoring his question.

"She's not," he scoffed. She was amusing. That was all. "And you never gave me an answer."

His friend sighed. "You'd have to ask Dr. Mak'en for the specifics, but I believe it's because there were no other viable female subjects. Only men have been experimented on as part of soldier programs."

"Then why was she?"

"Her father insisted she be the first trial of it happening in utero."

"That is quite a gamble. What if something had gone wrong? Did the mother know?"

Aerue shrugged. "Does it matter?"

"Does she know what she is?"

"Do you think she'd be asking why we took her if she did?"

"She could be testing us. You can't underestimate her, Aerue."

"And you'd be smart not to overestimate her. She's still only human, Knox. If that changes—"

"When," he corrected.

"*When* that changes, don't think too much about her. You need to stay focused."

He rolled his eyes. "I've been focused on this project for a long time." A millennia, give or take a century. "That's not going to change because of a single human."

His friend nodded. "Glad to hear it, Your Majesty. Is there anything else you need from me tonight?"

Knox shook his head. "I'm going to bed. You should, too, since we have a big day tomorrow."

"I'll guard you."

"You haven't slept in as long as I have. You must be exhausted.

Let Dhaca handle the night shift. All the other humans are already sleeping so there shouldn't be any issues. That's an order," he added before his friend could argue.

His friend sighed. "Yes, Your Majesty. Sleep well."

"Goodnight, Aerue. I'll see you tomorrow." He walked to the throne and lightly touched the back's center. The wall behind the throne opened and he stepped into his private chambers.

He got undressed and lay down. It had been a good day, and tomorrow already promised to be better.

5

VERITY

VERITY COUNTED her steps as she was walked into a doorless and windowless room. To even get into the space, the guard had merely stared at a spot on the wall before it opened up from the center like a pixelated hologram breaking down. There wasn't a bed but a single chair. She was wondering how she was expected to sleep when the man who'd clocked her—Eiz'm—walked in and the wall closed up behind him, trapping them together.

She'd been expecting to go to bed, but now she understood what was happening. Still bound and now trapped, there wasn't anything she could do. Except maybe move in circles to evade him. But she couldn't even figure out how to open the door. If she hadn't seen the wall open with her own eyes, she would assume that there truly was no exit because there were no visible seams.

She sat down and waited.

He looked so much harsher than the guys she'd been left with in the throne room. And if she hadn't seen him be dismissed, she would've assumed he was the one running things on the ship.

"I have a few questions for you, and you're going to answer them, Verity."

"Only friends get to call me by my first name." The rebuke was out before she could catch it.

His eyes narrowed. "Miss Landau, then."

He knew her full name. Which meant that they had targeted her, and likely every captive on the ship. Their victims weren't random, which only made finding a connection between her and the others more important. It was the best clue to what they—she refused to think of them as aliens—were up to.

"How old are you?"

"What's it to you?"

"Your age," he said, his tone brooking no argument.

He was going to get one, anyway. But he had proven meaner than anyone else she'd met, so she wouldn't antagonize him anymore—or, at least try to. Which left her with silently protesting the question by not answering.

"Birth date."

As if she'd fall for that. Even on Earth, knowing someone else's birthdate gave you a much better chance of learning more secure information about them. The only thing more telling that wasn't biological like DNA, a fingerprint, or an iris scan was your social security number. She doubted the aliens had those for themselves but she wouldn't put it past them to have found some way to access America's databases if they raided Groom Lake so easily.

"Siblings?"

She just stared at him impassively.

"Mother? We both already know about your father."

Verity bit her lip hard to prevent from lashing out at him for the well-aimed barb.

When she refused to be baited, he grabbed the front of her shirt, jerking her close enough for her to bite him if she thought she had a chance of getting away with it. "When I ask a question, I expect an answer." He raised his fist and was about to strike her when the door popped open, revealing the head guard's silhouette.

"Eiz'm!" the man reprimanded. "She wasn't to be interrogated tonight. And no harm is to come to her."

Then why had the guards brought her here? Was Eiz'm acting on his own? Why would he do that?

The better question was why was the guy in the throne room so concerned with her not being hurt? He'd been pissed about the split lip, too. Since when did captors care about the physical safety of their victims? Unless she was going to be ransomed?

Verity was jerked out of her thoughts when her temporary savior hustled her out into the corridor and quickly walked her to another room. She barely had time to count the number of doors before she saw the tiniest bathroom she'd ever seen. There was just enough space for her to slide between the sink and sit on the toilet, and not much else. Good thing she had never been claustrophobic. She looked at the guard holding her chains. The other two stood around her creating a wall with their bodies, cutting off any possible escape. If she couldn't run, there was no reason to have her hands tied while she went to the bathroom.

"Go," he grunted when she didn't move.

She flexed her hands, drawing his attention to the fact they were still shackled. He undid them and practically pushed her inside.

She waited until the wall closed. She had no idea if they could see through the walls, but if they expected her to do anything, she needed privacy.

When she was she was done, she knocked on the wall, hoping the guard could hear it on the other side. He must have because an instant later, she was released from the room and just as quickly detained again as the restraints were reapplied.

The guards led her further down the hall until they came to another stop. The wall opened and revealed the small quarters she would be staying in. It was the size of a large bathroom but it lacked a toilet. At least it had a bed, though it didn't look comfortable enough to deserve the title. It was a cot that was maybe three-inches thick. And that was being generous. It didn't look like a comfortable material but she looks could be deceiving. On the mattress, a plain top and pants were folded and a toothbrush. A pair of slippers were under the bed.

He took her shackles off then left. The door closed, trapping her inside all alone.

She checked every surface and corner of the room—not that there were many aside from a shelf attached to the wall across from the bed—for any type of camera or recording device and came up empty. Though she didn't believe for a moment that they weren't watching her. They would be stupid not to. But she was too tired to anything but sleep at this point. Hopefully they'd feed her breakfast. Then she'd figure out a plan.

THE BURST of air woke her, jolting her upright on the uncomfortable plank and barely-there mattress that had been her bed. Two guards stood expectantly outside her door. She swung her legs over, put on the slippers, and followed them out. Again, she counted their progress by passing doors, though this time, there were a few more twists and turns on their journey. She was led into a mess hall of sorts filled with the other captives sitting down at different tables, and the walls were filled with watching guards.

One of her escorts plopped her down at a table and released her shackles while the other walked away. When he returned with a filled bowl and a glass of what she assumed was water, they both left to join their eleven other comrades who held their position agains the wall in a circle around the room, hemming them in like animals. It was demeaning, to say the least.

One saw her looking and took a menacing step forward. She averted her eyes to her lunch mate.

The only bright side to the whole situation was Ben was at the same table. In fact, it was just the two of them, which was strange since the others were split into tables of four. The ones who had been singled out weren't present. And she hadn't seen Tristan since he was taken away. Maybe he was being interrogated? Which was incredibly inhumane to do before the first meal of the day, but then again, these weren't *humans* they were talking about. Who knew what code these aliens lived by? If they lived by one at all, aside from the clear military and chain of command she'd glimpsed in her short time on board.

Ben's gaze immediately dropped to her mouth, and her stomach flipped.

When she was younger, she sometimes daydreamed about what it would be like to kiss him, but those days were behind her. At least, she'd though they were. He'd never shown any interest in her before, but maybe he'd been holding back?

"What happened to you?" he asked.

Verity wanted to smack herself. Of course he wasn't attracted to her. That would be stupid. She was the General's daughter, and no one in their right mind would ever cross that line.

"I didn't cooperate last night." She examined him and saw a bruise on his temple. "Looks like you didn't either."

"One of the bastards blindsided me."

She bet it was Eiz'm, but she couldn't ask because she had no idea if he knew any of their names. She wondered if he knew anything at all. Except for the obvious fact of them being held by inhuman captors.

"So, what happened?"

"They burst into the dorms and we started fighting them. But we had no warning whatsoever. I have no idea how they did it."

"I saw lights and heard noise."

"Yeah, the base security finally kicked in. Can't say it helped."

She'd heard the alarm go off *after* she had already been woken up. What would Ben say if she told him that? She didn't think he'd call her delusional, but she still didn't want to chance it. So, she didn't correct him.

Instead, she glanced down at her plate, then back up at him. As far as she could tell, it looked like a mushy bowl of oatmeal. It didn't look appetizing. "Have you tried it yet?"

He shook his head. "I don't trust it. I can't believe you're even considering eating it. I thought you would be better than that."

"What are you going to do? Starve yourself until they give you a better option?"

"Better that than risk being poisoned."

"If they wanted to kill us, they would've already. Why kidnap us at all if it was just to kill us? And I don't think that's their goal. The one who gave me this," she gestured to her cut lip, "got reprimanded for doing so. For some reason, they don't want us hurt."

"I think they don't want *you* hurt. No one said anything when I was inspected last night."

So, she wasn't that special after all. Everyone had met the guy last night. Though if Ben was right and they didn't want her injured, then maybe she was still special. But why?

She took a spoonful and examined it. It didn't look dangerous. And she was absolutely starving. She opened her mouth to take a bite, but the doors opened suddenly, surprising her. She put the spoon down as the head guard from last night strode in, an annoyed expression on his features. "You."

She didn't move.

He reached her. "Let's go. The king wants a word with you."

The King? What did he want with her? She hadn't even met him. She met Ben's inquisitive expression and shrugged in response to his unanswered question. She had no idea what this was about either.

The alien hauled her up from the bench and led her through the hall until she was back in the throne room as last night. And sitting at the head of a long dining table was the same guy she'd verbally sparred with last night. It would be just her luck that he would be the king, the top of the power chain in this floating metal box. She'd definitely gotten that wrong last night.

He lifted his glass to salute her. "I told you I'd see you again."

Verity forced a smile. "You did." Her eyes drifted to the floor to ceiling windows on the left side of the room. She walked around the table to look outside at the inky night. Looking down, she spotted a very familiar giant red spot. How had they traveled so far so fast? She gasped then turned and saw that he was standing next to her. She hadn't even heard him approach. "So," she said in what she hoped was an even tone, "you're the king?"

"I am. My name is Knox." He indicated the chair on the right of the one where he'd been when she entered the room. "Sit."

She bit back a retort about not being a dog and did as she was told. "You don't wear a crown? If I'd known who you were, I would've been nicer last night," she said, surveying the table. He had a chrome goblet filled with bright blue liquid, a color she had only seen in the Caribbean Sea. She had a matching cup filled with clear liquid. Was it water or something else, something more dangerous? If it was poison, it was odorless and colorless, leaving her nothing to go on other than the hope that she had been right when she told Ben the aliens didn't want to kill them. Or, at the very least, that the king hadn't changed his mind about keeping her alive.

His plate was filled with green and purple foods she'd never seen before and instead of the same food as the mess hall, her plate here had eggs and bacon. Or, something that looked like it. She looked up to find him watching her.

"It's water and the food is real," he said, answering her unspoken questions. "And I'm not sure I believe that. You don't seem the type to bow down to authority."

"Well, you're right about one thing. I don't bow to anyone. We don't have royalty in my country. How do you have human food?"

"So, you do believe that I'm not human? You were very skeptical last night during our last discussion. What changed?"

Shit. She should've stuck with pretending to be ignorant and disbelieving. If he found out how much she knew, he'd keep digging for information to hurt her and who knew what else. Why couldn't she control herself around this guy? "Answer the question." And now she'd just given a king an order. A king who held her life in his hands. Absolutely genius.

It wasn't that she had an overarching issue with authority—her dad had always been fair with his discipline—but there was something about this alien king that got under her skin and obliterated her polite filter. Her dad had always said her smart mouth would get her in trouble one day. She just hoped that it wasn't today. Truth be told, she wasn't as confident in her safety as she had told Ben. The king might have told his man Eiz'm off for hurting her, but that didn't mean Knox wouldn't do it himself, right? She needed to be careful.

"It's not that hard to manufacture," he answered. His tone was plain and disinterested as if his kind's easy engineering of Earth's food was no big deal. Maybe it wasn't. But if it were that easy for them, what else could they do? "Your planet's resources aren't that different from ours."

It was the first piece of information he'd given about his background. She wracked her brain for any planet mentioned in her multiple astronomy classes that was both Earth-like and was said to be able to support life but came up empty. Sure, there had been planets that fit the first criterion, and others that potentially fit the latter, but she couldn't think of one that scientists had determined capable of supporting intelligent life—much less life that so closely resembled humans.

But maybe he was lying. It's not like she could fact check him. He might be deceiving her right now, but she believed him when he said he was an alien. She trusted him about that, if nothing else. Even if someone had brought up the possibility of a hostile power having the capability of doing what his people had done, something about them hadn't felt human when she was fighting them.

When she didn't speak, he asked, "How did you sleep?"

Were they really making small talk? The king had specially invited her to talk about insignificant things? Bullshit. He was probably fishing and didn't want to be too obvious.

"Fine." She took the spoon and pushed the egg around, searching for anything hidden inside, like maybe a pill or powder. Nothing.

Her stomach growled.

He gave her a knowing look and she scowled. He seemed way too satisfied knowing that she couldn't resist.

She took a bite, and was surprised at how good it was. If he was telling the truth, she expected the ingredients to be similar enough to what she was used to, but she assumed the cook or machine that made the food would've somehow botched the preparation. But these eggs were light and fluffy and not too salty. Perfect. Which only made her more wary of these aliens. Had they secretly been creating and modifying food on Earth? If they had, to what end? And why was she only coming up with more and more questions but no answers or a way to get them. The *king* clearly wasn't going to come clean if last night was any indication.

"You don't look happy. Is it not to your liking?"

"If I say yes, will you send it back to the kitchen?"

He chuckled and shook his head.

"Then why ask?"

He shrugged. "Curiosity."

"Curiosity killed the cat."

"I've heard this saying before, though I don't fully understand why it's been perpetuated. They seem like quite a fearful species to me. Regardless," he smiled, "it's a good thing I'm not a cat, then, isn't it?"

For fuck's sake! He was witty, too? If he hadn't ordered her kidnapping, she'd maybe like him. She just had to remember why not to because if she let herself forget, she'd be in trouble.

"I don't know where it came from. There are lots of sayings that seem to come from nowhere." It was such a strangely mundane topic to be on, but sharing anything about her language —and therefore humanity—felt like a betrayal of her planet.

"What's another?"

"I can't think of any right now," she lied. She was definitely thinking of a few that would make her dad reprimand her for even thinking, and it would probably surprise the STFs to learn that she even had them in her vocabulary. "If you're trying to butter me up with food so I'll give you answers, it's not going to work." She took another bite of the eggs. She still didn't trust the bacon.

He opened his mouth to reply, but he was cut off before he could start when the doors opened revealing a beautiful woman.

"I wanted to see what was keeping you and my brother busy." The woman's gaze scanned the room then landed on her.

Verity sat up straighter. Who was this woman who set the king on edge? Was she his mother? Probably not based on her age. Then again, she'd thought that Knox was too young to be king so maybe she was wrong. But if she wasn't his mother, was she his wife? Or sister? Whatever her title, she was probably royalty and therefore likely had a say in her fate.

"Is she one of them?"

"Arfilmea," he hissed out. "I told you I wanted privacy."

Verity glanced between the two of them. Did this woman really not know? Verity hadn't seen the whole ship yet, but she doubted it was large enough for this stranger to not notice the eighteen humans who had become unwilling guests last night. And despite this alien race's similarities to humanity, if the ones she'd met were average, the average alien was taller than the average human, which immediately should've ruled her out as anything but a human with her five-and-a-half-foot stature. It had never bothered her too much before, but now she felt tiny.

The newcomer ignored the king's comment and sat down on his other side, facing Verity head on. "I've never seen you before. I take it you're human?"

"Yes," she said. There was no point in denying it.

She'd told herself she'd come up with a plan this morning, but she now was at a complete loss. She'd never felt more vulnerable in her life than in the presence of these two—three if you counted the guard—aliens who could likely kill her without blinking an eye.

6

KNOX

KNOX GLARED AT ARFILMEA, but she didn't flinch under his stare. Instead, she reclined in her chair with a small smile on her face, looking entirely too comfortable given she was an uninvited guest. And she was staring at Verity with far too much interest for his liking. Like she was a puzzle to solve. And she was. But she was *his* puzzle to solve, and no one else's. He wasn't going to share her, and certainly not with Arfilmea.

The door opened and a plate full of food was placed in front of her. Clearly, she'd warned some people of her arrival but not him or her brother. Not that he should be surprised. She liked to live as if she were in charge and keep the two of them in the dark. She said it was to keep them humble, but if anyone needed humbling, it was her.

He needed to have a talk with his staff about disregarding his orders in favor of staying in her good graces. They weren't hers to command and their loyalty was clearly lacking.

"So, what's your name?"

Verity glanced at him before regarding her warily. "You don't already know?"

Her assumption that Arfilmea would know was wrong but

not completely misguided. He already had information on all the subjects thanks to Trohm but the interviews were to confirm and gain new information that could aid them in their mission. He doubted whether she knew that, but it would take an idiot to not realize Eiz'm was reporting to him. And Verity was no idiot. But she underestimated the compartmentalization of information.

Arfilmea only needed to know things that directly involved her, and therefore was mostly oblivious about the project. She only knew the broad concepts of the plan, not the particulars of how it was being carried out. Or, at least he'd thought so. She seemed to have gotten information out of someone to know that he was eating breakfast with Verity.

Arfilmea shook her head. "Knox doesn't tell me anything anymore." He turned away from Verity to see his friend smile sadly. And not in her manipulative way that she did in order to gain sympathy. She seemed to be genuinely mourning their lost intimacy. "We used to be closer when we were younger."

Which to Verity would be millions of years ago.

"How old are you?" Verity shot back, deftly avoiding the need to answer the first question.

Arfilmea didn't seem to notice and leaned forward. "Don't you humans have a rule about not asking a woman her age?"

"*Knox* keeps insisting none of you are human, so I didn't think it applied to you."

Why did he like hearing her finally say his name? He hadn't intentionally withheld it from her, but it was nice for them to now be able to converse on a first-name basis.

"How old are you?" Arfilmea fired back.

Eiz'm had failed to confirm Trohm's information during his unsanctioned interrogation of her last night, but Knox already knew that Verity was twenty-two years old. He had no idea why his colonel had acted of his own accord, but he wouldn't have minded as much if it had yielded results. He was still unhappy that Eiz'm had been on the verge of violence when Aerue discovered them. That would've been twice that Verity was harmed by Eiz'm, and if what the reading had said was accurate—she had to be treated carefully, more so than any of the others.

Verity sighed and muttered, "Twenty-two."

He turned back toward her. His best interrogator couldn't get this human to cough up a single biographical detail but *Arfilmea* could? What was happening here?

"That's still considered young in a human lifespan, yes?"

"Yep."

"And most humans start having children around this stage of life, yes?"

Verity startled in her seat, almost knocking over his drink.

He steadied the glass and shot a glare at his best friend's sister. If she wasn't careful, she'd give too much away, and regardless of Verity's unexpected cooperation, he had no doubt that she would take any information she could gather and turn it against them at the first opportunity. They'd entered her life as the enemy, and as a General's daughter, she was likely well versed in war and spy tactics. She was certainly skilled in fighting according to the soldiers' individual reports. She succeeded where her father hadn't, and that only further proved that she was exactly what they'd been looking for.

"Um, no," Verity answered, uncharacteristically hesitant. "Not the majority, at least." She recovered quickly. "That hasn't been the standard for a few decades. Do you have children?"

Arfilmea laughed. "Oh, no. I'm not rushing towards motherhood anytime soon." She gave him an arch look as she answered.

He frowned. They'd already talked about this, but it seemed he needed to remind her of her responsibility and duties to their kind. He wasn't looking forward to it any more than she was, but they didn't have the luxury of neglecting their species' dire situation.

Knox motioned Aerue forward. This conversation was clearly moving in the wrong direction and he needed to end it before it did too much damage. "Have someone take your sister back to her room." He could have easily had him leave, but he seemed to be the only one to keep Verity in check and protect her from Eiz'm, as well as him from her although it was still largely unnecessary.

Arfilmea pouted. "But I don't want to leave," she said in a soft and childlike voice. As if he'd fall for that trick. He hadn't for the past few millennia, though that didn't stop her from trying it whenever she really wanted something. "I'm having so much fun chatting with your special guest."

He didn't like how intensely she was watching Verity. He was doing the same, but seeing her do it bothered him for some unknown reason. It's not like she had malevolent intentions or could do her any harm. He had been very clear to everyone that humans were not to be irreparably damaged under any circumstances, even in interrogation, and Arfilmea had nothing to do with those proceedings. But the invisible tension between the women still bothered him on a gut level.

He didn't dignify her non-request with an answer. The more attention he paid her, the longer she'd stay. "I don't care where you take her, just get her out of here."

Aerue nodded and quickly stepped out of the room. A moment later, a guard appeared and escorted the stubborn woman out. Once she became his wife, he doubted he'd be able to get his men to aid him in managing their queen. They barely did the job now, and they weren't even married yet.

His friend came back, and Knox turned his attention back to Verity who had silently watched the scene play out.

"Who was that?"

"You already heard her name."

"Yes, but who **is** she? To you, specifically? She said you used to be close friends."

It seemed Arfilmea's intense interest wasn't unidirectional. "She's Aerue's sister."

Verity rolled her eyes. "Funnily enough, I got that on my own, too. There's something else going on between you two. I just can't figure out what it is."

She was relentless. No wonder Arfilmea liked her. She probably saw herself in Verity and assumed they could be friends. Which was impossible. His plan might involve the union of humans and Eochrons but there could never be *friendship*, especially given Verity's correct assessment that Earth saw their actions as an act of war. No, they would not become friends. The humans were a means to the end and forming attachments to them was not smart.

Even if it were a possibility, he wasn't sure he wanted these women getting close to each other, anyway. They'd likely gang up on him and he'd never again have any peace. He shuddered at the idea. He needed to keep them separate from now on.

"She's my betrothed," he finally admitted. Not by choice. And though their fathers were both dead, therefore eliminating the only people who could enforce the union, neither he nor Arfilmea could deny the necessity of it. And it could be worse. At least they both cared about each other to understand the other's position and ultimately preserve their independence. He wouldn't have to worry about her constantly clinging to him given her general disinterest in politics despite her father having been his father's most senior advisor.

Verity didn't verbally respond. In fact, she seemed at a loss for words. Though why his relationship with Arfilmea would affect her so much was a puzzle.

"Satisfied now?" he asked. He took a sip of his energy serum. It was derived from elements unknown to Earth and provided much more sustenance and benefits than human coffee or tea.

She was watching him when he finished and put the goblet down. Caught, she glanced out the window and shrugged, aloof once more. "Did you pick each other? I only ask because you don't seem...very affectionate towards one another."

He wasn't about to share the complicated details about him and Arfilmea. If she knew that they weren't pleased about being engaged, Verity would no doubt try to use that to sow political unrest among his kind. Not that it would matter. As long as they went through with it and had a few children, everyone would be satisfied. Except, maybe, Arfilmea, but again, she knew what needed to be done and had promised to do her part. He was working on his project to help with the issue, but it was unlikely it would be ready soon enough for them to have the option of calling off the union.

Verity smiled, taking his silence as an answer on its own.

They continued eating until their plates were clean. She had eventually eaten the meat, despite being suspicious all throughout the meal. Only then did he summon Aerue from his post at the door again.

"Please personally make sure Miss Landau makes it to her room. I don't want any detours again."

"Of course." Aerue refastened her bindings and led her out of the dining room.

Knox stood, opened the secret passage to avoid running into Verity, and went in search of Arfilmea. He didn't want her having contact with the humans until they were ready, but if he couldn't prevent that, he needed to know that she would behave well and not jeopardize everything he'd worked for and the future of their species. She could be entitled, but she'd never crossed the line before. He wouldn't allow her to start now.

He found her in the library, lounging sideways in his favorite chair. She likely did it on purpose to irk him.

She didn't bother to close her reading or look up at him. "Bored with the human already?"

Not even remotely. "That's not why I'm here."

"Yes, yes, I know. You're here to reprimand me for having contact with one of them without your express permission. See? I just saved you the time it took to get here. You can run on back to your pet human now."

"Don't think you're getting off that easily."

"Nothing is easy with you," she shot back, still not meeting his gaze.

He waved his hand, dissolving the text in front of her. He needed her full attention. "That, and you clearly forgetting that you will become a mother sooner rather than later. You told me you understood that, and yet you told her that you have no intention of doing it on the timeline we agreed."

"If we're going to talk about my reproductive system like it's your property, I'd appreciate it if you weren't talking down to me. Sit down, why don't you?"

He raised an eyebrow at her. She sighed and moved her legs so he could take the spot next to her.

"Better?" he asked.

She tucked her heels under herself so she was sitting on them and turned toward him. "I don't know why you're rushing this. It's not like we're going to die out tomorrow if you don't have an heir in a few months. We're not even rushing the wedding."

"Because neither of us wanted to."

She looked down at her skirt and smoothed out an imaginary wrinkle. "And I don't want a child right now but it seems like that doesn't matter to you."

Her eyes raised to meet his again and he felt a pang of regret pierce him. She wasn't totally wrong. "You know it does, but I can't be selfish and neither can you. You know I wouldn't ask you if there was another way." Even if his plan worked better than his desired outcome, he still needed a pureblood heir to placate those who were opposed to his idea. Even Arfilmea would likely side with them on the issue even if she wasn't against the rest of his project.

"It can wait a bit longer, but I wouldn't get used to the idea that you'll have a few more years before we need to handle it."

"You make it sound so romantic."

"We both know we don't feel that way about each other."

She didn't answer. "I'll do what my king commands, but as a friend, please put it off as long as possible. Our lives will change afterwards and I'm not ready for that. Being Queen has rules I'm not ready for."

He doubted she'd ever be ready to follow any rules but he nodded all the same. "I'll do my best."

"Thank you." She leaned forward and kissed his cheek. "I promise I'll be on my best behavior around the humans from now on. Can I go back to my reading or are you going to lecture me some more?"

He gave her a pointed look.

"I'll be on my best behavior and avoid the humans from now on," she amended.

"Good. And please don't bribe the guards or scientists or whomever you got your information from. I'd hate to punish them for breaking confidence because you wheedled it out of them."

She smiled. "Maybe you should. If they can't resist me, how will they stand up to an enemy?"

He rolled his eyes. "Arfilmea."

"All right," she conceded. "But you're taking away all my fun. What will I have left?"

"I'm sure you'll find other ways to entertain yourself."

"You know I'm not interested in any of them."

He shrugged. "There's still a chance you'll get bored enough to change your mind."

She hit him lightly. "Get out."

"You're kicking me out of my own library?"

"Yes."

He stood. "Don't get used to it."

"If anyone is adjusting to a new normal, I think it'll be you. I'm becoming your queen, remember?"

"I'm sorry to say our society will not become a matriarchy just because I've married you."

He took a step back to avoid being hit by the archival tome she launched at him. "I'll see you at dinner," he said. "Don't be late."

She didn't answer.

He turned and walked to the control room. His guards been questioning the humans since breakfast which had ended while he was still dining with Verity. By now, some of them should have moved into the next stage of their day: the stress test for the subjects' natural baseline capacity to deal with extreme physical conditions. The results would be used in comparison to subsequent tests once the treatment started taking effect.

He pictured Verity's reaction at being brought into the testing chamber and smiled. She would no doubt make a few quips about being treated like a lab rat. In a way, they were, though there would be no withholding of food or shocks administered to the human subjects.

Taking a seat, he pulled up the surveillance of the first human and listened to what he had to say. It wasn't a long conversation, and soon the human was quickly spouting words, most of which were nonsensical. Knox sighed. This one didn't appear to know anything useful.

He saw the indicator that a new recording had just been processed and clicked on it: the interrogation of Captain Benjamin Tenner. Knox leaned forward and hit play. This should be interesting.

7

VERITY

"SO, *AERUE*," Verity began, as she walked in front of him down the same corridor as last night. "Who are you?"

While she waited for his answer, she counted her steps yet again. This time she wasn't going to the interrogation room first, and she needed to visualize every room for the map of the ship she had forming in her mind. She was at one hundred and thirteen already, and the hand at her back made it clear she wasn't going to be stopping anytime soon. They had just passed where the prisoner dining hall was, so they were getting closer to her room.

Maybe they'd let her change. She was still wearing her pajamas from last night and though she sometimes liked to lounge around in them on a lazy weekend, being forced to wear the same clothes due to the lack of any alternative wasn't fun.

"I think you can figure it out," Aerue muttered.

"The king's future brother-in-law and his current personal guard." But that wasn't much to go on. And who could blame her for asking? The hallway was absolutely silent, and she hated it. Not even her own footsteps made a sound. She needed noise.

He grunted in affirmation.

If she didn't know he was behind her, she'd be at a severe disadvantage. Which was so different from how she was normally hyperaware of people's presence by sound and smell even before she could see them. Normally, it was overwhelming so she almost always had music or something else on in the background. The only time she didn't was when she had class or was sleeping.

She looked over her shoulder in time to catch him frowning before he wiped his face of all emotions. "Why was I invited to breakfast with him when all the other captives ate in that dining hall?" Were they still there? Probably not since it was probably over an hour ago since she sat down with Ben to eat. Granted, she never took more than twenty minutes to eat, and the squadron was trained to eat even faster just in case they needed to move at a moment's notice.

He didn't answer. She wondered if Knox had told him to be stoic and unresponsive to her questions, or if it was an inherent trait in their species. Based on Arfilmea's expressiveness, she was going to guess it was the former.

She faced forward again and kept walking. "Why are you kidnapping humans, anyway? Your king never explained that to me in the two times I've met him." Not that he ever would. But she wouldn't stop asking until she got an answer. Besides, even with his silent act, she could feel some level of annoyance starting to radiate off her escort.

"Are you always this talkative?" His tone was as flat but as ever but the words were drawn out a bit, as if he were measuring them to avoid any inflection.

"Not really," she said lightly. At home, she was actually pretty quiet unless she was with friends. And given that group included a bunch of STFs, there wasn't much choice for her to be anything but loud if she didn't want to be drowned out by their chatter.

But there were definitely times when she was content to just listen. Being on this ship was one of those times, but she had to get these aliens to talk and the only way to do that seemed to be to pepper them with questions until they got sick of it enough to start answering. She hadn't quite reached their breaking point, but she was seeing progress with her half-baked method of extracting information. Too bad she hadn't sat in on interrogation training. At least, not the parts where she did the questioning. And, after last night, she probably should have gone to more sessions where she learned how to withstand interrogation and torture. Her dad had never asked her to learn those skills, though it was odd in retrospect given how much he insisted she needed combat and weapons training. Neither of them expected her to be in any position where any other skills would be necessary. Clearly, she should have also been training for the scenario where she lost a fight, not just ones where she came out as the victor.

Without any hope of getting help from home, she had to play the hand she was dealt until she could figure out something better. And if that required talking nonstop until someone shut her up or decided to talk themself, so be it. Talking to Ben again would also be a huge help, but who knew when that would be? She wondered what room he was being kept in. She should've asked him at breakfast. Though, if he was also counting by the number of personal strides, she'd have to convert his long ones to her slightly shorter ones. Luckily, as a dancer, she paid more attention to that kind of thing than others. And there wasn't too large of a difference because despite their height difference, she had learned to walk with large steps—a must to keep up with her father when she was a child. Hopefully, she'd get the chance to find out where Ben was staying tomorrow, unless the *king* decided to yank her chain and have her keep him company again.

Someone stopped them in the hall and whispered to Aerue.

She listened in and thought she heard, "meet in the lab." Why they were talking about something so secretive in her language in front of her made no sense, but she wasn't about to let them know she could hear them. Maybe they'd slip up and she could learn something useful about what the aliens were planning for her and the other humans.

They reached her room and he waited for her to step inside before he unlocked the manacles. She'd have to eventually figure that out how he did that if she was ever going to escape. But she was getting ahead of herself. She still didn't even know what these aliens were. Not that getting their species name would make any difference since no one on Earth had even anticipated their existence, but it would make her feel less ridiculous than having to think of them as *aliens* all the time. The food conversation had kind of ruined her ability to think of them as generic people. For some reason, it felt like Knox had been pushing her to acknowledge the full truth, though why he should care what she thought made absolutely no sense. Which was pretty consistent with what she knew of him so far.

A set of folded clothes were sitting on her bed. She picked up the top and held it up against her. She couldn't tell without putting it on, but it seemed like it would fit. Same with the pants. And that's when she saw the underwear. They were plain and did not come with a matching bra. In fact, there was no bra at all.

She cursed. Of course, Knox would have noticed she wasn't wearing one. Her body wasn't exactly subtle in its reaction to him—even if she hated his guts for what he'd done to her and the people she cared about. She threw the clothes back down.

She paced her room, feeling more empathy than ever for every prisoner anywhere on Earth. She was definitely a prisoner, but she was certain there was more to it, and she could only assume it was for some scientific research. Knox had admitted they manufactured food, so why wouldn't they be doing other things in their laboratory? Aerue was on his way there now for some reason, so there had to be a good reason. Before they had kidnapped her and the other humans, they had to have been working on something else, right?

The wall opened without warning and a guard she'd never seen before stood on the other side, another set of shackles intended for her ready in hand. His uniform was a plain white except for an insignia. But it was different from the ones Eiz'm and Aerue wore. This was lacked any lines and was only made of circles. Clearly, the different symbols had meanings but she had no idea what. Maybe rank? But then why would Aerue's be the same as Eiz'm's when he clearly was in a higher position of power as the king's personal guard?

"I wouldn't change into your new clothes yet, Miss Landau," the new alien said. "You can change afterwards." He motioned for her to follow him.

She didn't move. "After what?"

He didn't answer other than stepping close enough to grab her arm and fasten the cuffs around her wrists behind her back. He pushed her out of the room and into the corridor.

She started counting her steps again as he led her to who knows where.

When they eventually stopped, she was brought into another small room with nothing other than what could only be described as a treadmill with a cup sitting on the rail.

She looked at the guard who nodded at her to step onto it.

Gingerly, she did, and held her breath as he placed a sticker over her heart.

His fingers didn't linger any longer than necessary, and he pulled away quickly. He handed her the drink.

She stared at the dark blue liquid. What the hell was that? She glanced up at him.

"If you don't drink it, I'll be forced to make you."

Well, okay then. She brought the cup to her lips and tipped it up, holding her breath to avoid tasting anything as the liquid slid down her throat. Surprisingly, there was no flavor at all, not even the artificial blueberry she'd been anticipating. Normally, she could still detect some hints even while suppressing her senses.

He took the cup then he left.

She glanced around the room for a camera or one-way glass, but couldn't find anything strange. Stranger than a room with nothing but an exercise machine, that is. If she stepped off it, would something happen? What if she took off the sticker? She reached to do so, then almost tripped because in an instant, the track started moving. Her body's muscle memory kicked in, and she started walking. It was a slow pace, but if this was what she thought it was, it wouldn't stay that way for long.

It got faster, and now she was walking at her normal speed, which was faster than most of her civilian classmates on campus, but on par with the STFs and other military personnel she was usually surrounded by.

Again, the pace picked up and though she could feel her footfalls get slightly heavier to keep up, she was still breathing easily and didn't feel like she was exerting more energy than normal.

The speed incrementally increased at shorter and shorter intervals until eventually she was sprinting. She was panting now and cursing her alien captors enough to make her STF friends congratulate her. Even as a dancer, there was nothing she hated more than cardio. If she was going to be sweating, it was going to be a means to an end. Learning how to fight and defend herself? Fine. Learning a new dance or performing said dance for an audience? Cool. But just to get her heart rate up or for the sake of exercise itself? Pass.

Clearly, she wasn't only a rat in a maze but also beholden to the whims and orders of others for the amusement of a certain, infuriating alien king. She still couldn't figure out the research reasons he would need a bunch of humans for. A stress test was for people's heart health and from the people she'd seen kidnapped with her, no one seemed to be at risk of heart failure of any kind. Then why was being forced to run like a hamster on a wheel?

By the time the machine rolled to a stop, a light sheen of

sweat coated her skin, causing her tank top to cling to her and no doubt showed more than she wanted it to. The wall opened again and the same guard held out the manacles for her. She sighed and walked up to him, wrists crossed behind her back.

As he fastened them, she asked, "Can I at least shower?"

"I'll take you to bathe now. You'll have time to change into your new clothes before lunch."

Her life was apparently now only existing from meal to meal except when she was being yanked out of her room for some sort of torture. Joy of joys. What she wouldn't give to be stuck in conditioning class with the STFs. It was one of the few times they didn't throw quips around with every breath, but just being around them always made the experience more enjoyable. Misery loved company, but their presence also lightened every scenario she'd ever been in.

He walked her through the corridor, passing where she mentally marked the minuscule bathroom's location and the dining hall. But when they walked further than the entrance to her room, she started counting her steps again. She was now entering unmarked territory of the ship's layout.

They stopped in front of what turned out to be a single glass chamber. Hopefully it was a shower and not a modern, alien version of a certain genocidal German's favorite way to kill people.

"You wanted to wash off," the guard explained.

But where was she supposed to get undressed? There was no way in hell she was going to strip in front of him, in the middle of the hall, where anyone could see if they walked by. Bad enough that there was likely a hidden camera in her room and everywhere else on the ship, but to be so blatantly confronted with the reality that she was being watched was taking it too far.

"Do you mind?" she snapped.

The guard lifted an eyebrow.

Maybe he didn't understand the concept of privacy, didn't

think humans deserved it, or didn't understand that's what she was implying. All of them meant she was forced to explicitly spell it out for him.

"Are you going to watch me undress or is there somewhere I can do that that's not in the shower?" She was going to assume it was a cleaning chamber. Like she told Ben, if Knox and his people wanted them dead, they already would be. "Or maybe a towel?" Which she'd also need to dry off, and to wear something on the way back to her room where the new clothes awaited her.

Thank goodness she hadn't worn her favorite pajamas last night because she was pretty sure she'd never be seeing them again once she took them off.

The guard rolled his eyes, unlocked her cuffs, and turned his back.

Verity sighed. That was clearly the best offer she'd be getting.

She closed her eyes, blocking out the guard watching her, and stripped down. She kicked the clothes to the floor and stepped into the chamber. When she opened them again, she was enclosed in the space, the wall having reformed in the moment she wasn't looking.

There was absolutely no warning before water began to pour down from above. She glanced up through the water dripping down her eyelashes and saw there were minuscule holes in the ceiling. They were so closely packed together that rather than feeling like individual streams, they merged until it felt like she was standing under a waterfall.

She needed soap, and no sooner had she thought it, she noticed a small spout in the wall. Curious, she placed her hand under it and foam filled her hand.

Verity quickly washed herself, skipping shampooing her hair. She didn't feel like playing roulette in guessing whether the body wash could also be used on her scalp.

After a few moments of not moving at all, the water shut off and she was blasted with air from all sides. It was so sudden she didn't have time to feel cold before she was completely dry, eliminating the internal-external temperature difference.

There must have been another sensor because as soon as all the water was evaporated off her skin, the air shut off. When nothing else happened, she knocked on the wall and waited.

The guard stood there and handed her a towel.

He couldn't have done that *before* she got undressed? It's not like she needed it now to dry off. Even her hair was taken care of. And it normally took her 20 minutes to dry with a blow-dryer. Whatever. It was a moot point now. And it was something to shield her body, so there was that.

They walked back to her room. Despite the embarrassingly scant outfit, she kept her head up. Once she was inside the threshold, he left her alone.

She changed into the plain clothes, then lay down and stared at the ceiling. A short nap sounded heavenly, and with nothing else to do, why not? She closed her eyes and waited for sleep to take her.

8

KNOX

KNOX SAT WAITING in a large chair while Dr. Mak'en was conversing with one of her assistants. When he'd arrived, Aerue wasn't there, and he'd told them to wait for his guard before starting the presentation. He wasn't expecting any trouble from any of the humans, but one of the guards had told him after breakfast that the Captain had been markedly agitated once Verity had left. He'd asked them to explain more and all they could say was they had been talking alone at a table when Aerue had come in.

He'd watched a recording of their conversation and heard them discussing how his soldiers had raided their base and the likelihood of his kind poisoning them. What was most interesting was Verity admitting that she heard and saw signs of their ship before they had infiltrated her home. Only his kind could see through their cloaking technology and for a human to be able to—even a genetically modified one—was unexpected.

Aerue finally arrived and the lead scientist walked over.

"We've finished analyzing and sorting the biological samples collected from the subjects, Your Majesty. There's a wide range in their numbers. I was expected more uniformity among the subjects based on your scouts' surveillance." Her tone held a little censure but he was inclined to agree. If the lowest numbers were that far removed from the highest, it was going to take a lot longer to prepare all the subjects for the next phase.

Verity and her Captain had rightly been worried during breakfast, but they had focused on the wrong perceived threat. In addition to keeping them alive, breakfast had been an opportunity for them to non-invasively gather much needed information for their project.

"As you can see, Your Majesty, we've ranked the different features of each subject, and we can reconfigure the sorting by any factor you wish."

"I only care about one." She had finally been given her first stress test and, as he suspected, she had excelled not just when compared to the non-soldier humans but was almost on par with her Captain. Strange, given she wasn't subject to the same rigorous training routine as him.

She nodded. "Of course. If you look here," she eliminated multiple columns until the name, age, and most important statistic remained for each data entry.

At the bottom, fourteen of them were showing less than ten percent of hybridization with Eochronian DNA. The remaining four were more promising, though there were still gaps rather than linear progress: eleven, twenty-four, thirty-seven, and lastly fifty-three-percent. Trohm's suspicion and Eiz'm's preliminary scan of Verity had proven correct. She had the highest percentage, but he was slightly surprised that the Captain was the second highest-ranked. Trohm had obviously confirmed he was a viable candidate before he sent his soldiers to the compound, but he had expected lower numbers from him given he hadn't shown as many signs as she had. He had just seen evidence of the discrepancy between their abilities from their conversation. Verity's bridging the gap was likely a result of her hybrid DNA.

"Is it enough to start the next phase?" he asked, zooming in on the surveillance captures of her during the stress test. Her blood glowed in her veins thanks to the dye and he could see her heart pumping in her chest as she started running.

He looked over at Aerue who stood by the door looking bored. His friend supported his plan but he made no effort in pretending to be interested in the particulars.

"We just put the finishing touches on a prototype serum with the human and hybrid DNA, but it hasn't been tested yet, Your Majesty. We're not ready for a full rollout at maximum capacity just yet, but we are ready to test on the subjects we have."

He looked away from the picture and swiveled in his chair to face Dr. Mak'en again. "What would you suggest?"

Her eyes darted to the recording before returning back to him. She cleared her throat. "We can either start with the lowest scores in attempts to increase them, or we could target the higher ones to potentially reach a completely viable specimen sooner rather than later. Of course, the latter method also has a larger risk because if there is a fault, it could render the subject obsolete."

Even if the affected subject didn't die, they couldn't afford to harm any of them. He pictured Verity and immediately knew there was only one choice.

"Start with the lower ones." He turned to leave, then paused. "And if there's a way to experiment on the higher ones in a conservative way, you could also start on the rest except for the top candidate. If anything jeopardizes her, I will not be happy. And I will personally hold you responsible for anything that happens to her. Understood?"

She lowered her gaze to the floor. "Yes, Your Majesty."

"Is there anything else?"

She shook her head.

He nodded and left, Aerue trailing behind him.

The door had barely closed behind them before his friend

asked, "Are you sure it's a good idea to extend it so far up the line?"

Knox kept walking. He wanted to review more footage of the test subjects. He fully trusted his scientist, but he still wanted to see the results for himself. "What are you implying?"

"If you didn't know about their relationship, would you really be willing to risk our two best chances?"

"But I'm not. I'm hedging bets on all of the subjects—conservatively, I should add— except on the best one. Therefore, you're wrong. If I was jeopardizing any of the subjects as you claim, it would only reach up to the second-best subject. Not both of 'our two best chances.'"

"You're splitting hairs. You know what I meant."

"And I'm telling you you're wrong. I know what I'm doing."

His friend didn't look convinced.

It didn't matter. He'd be checking in on the progress daily, and if anything was starting to go wrong, he'd tell them to dial it down so that only the weakest subjects would be affected before they lost all their prospects. The plan was going smoothly, and that was all that mattered. Soon, their population crisis would be solved. And once they were fully integrated with humans on Earth, they would also have a home once again.

There was nothing the humans could do to stop them, and the only thing that would derail it from their side would be an internal threat. And though Eiz'm had been a danger to Verity, that was resolved now and their pool of potential subjects would only grow as they scaled up.

"Where are you going now?" Aerue asked.

"I didn't realize I had to run my agenda by you. Did I sleep through myself naming you as my timekeeper?"

His friend didn't even crack a smile. "I was going to debrief the guards if you didn't need me."

"That's fine. I was going in the same direction to the guard room. I'd like some privacy there, so you can take them to the hangar or use the throne room. If I don't see you after that, I'll see you later at dinner with your sister."

They reached their destination and the thirteen guards who were manning the stations immediately stood at attention.

"I need the room. Follow Aerue out to be debriefed."

They bowed as one and said, "Yes, Your Majesty."

He sat down in the chair in the center of the room and waited as the guards filed out.

Picking up where he left off, he settled into the seat.

A scientist named Joseph was being interrogated by Dhaca.

"Age," his guard prompted.

"Thirty."

Knox leaned forward. He didn't look that old, even by human standards. He would have guessed early twenties, similar to Verity, rather than being the same age as the human Captain.

"And your job?"

"Junior scientist at ASE."

"What do you do?"

"I'm part of a team that helps calculate probabilities for and modifies digital models of the universe."

"Give me an example."

"I calculate the properties of exoplanets based on data and observations we receive from satellites and telescopes."

"And the farthest planet you've identified?"

"SWEEPS-04 and -11."

Knox smiled. Those planets were still much closer to Earth than his. Even with their highly advanced technology, traveling from Khavraid to Earth still took many Earth years.

If they hadn't been detected on the military base, Earth would be many years away from even discovering their planet—and only seeing it years after it had already been blown up by their enemies. His grandfather had been a war-hungry colonizer and while his father had been better, he had also made his fair share of enemies.

Before Earth, Knox had yet to do so, but even if Earth's power was nothing compared to his people's he was sure that he'd already made an enemy of the human race—at the very least, a very powerful sect of the species.

The rest of the interview proved to be rather boring. The man knew nothing of Earth's military's role in their collaboration with the space research and exploration organization beyond the fact that such a alliance existed in the first place.

"That information is highly compartmentalized, and I don't have clearance," he said.

Disappointing, but not totally unexpected. Perhaps they had better luck with interrogating the other military personnel they'd grabbed. If they were anything like the human Captain, they would be harder to get talking than those who had no training but if they didn't talk on their own, there were ways to get past that. Some more physical than others, but their human bodies were weak enough to not need advanced interrogation techniques they used on previous enemies.

The next interview proved him right as a young recruit was sat in the chair and started giving answers after a few false starts once Dhaca administered the special serum.

However, yet again, the human didn't know much. This time, while he was in the right organization, he was of too low a rank to be included in or privy to the plans regarding Earth and extraterrestrial interactions. It seemed only Verity and the human Captain knew much of anything and neither were inclined to talk.

The wall opened and Aerue stepped in. "Are you done? My men would like to get back to work."

Knox spun in the chair and leveled a look at his guard. "And if I wasn't?"

"They would have an extended break and no one would be monitoring the humans other than those being currently questioned or tested because we both know **you** are only interested in watching one."

"I'll let that slide, but watch your tone, Aerue. I might choose to promote Dhaca to your job."

"You'd never do such a thing. You like having someone call you out when necessary."

"I think you take a little too much pleasure in doing so." He would say the same thing about Verity. For all her teasing, Arfilmea never quite crossed over into criticism the way his friend and the human female did.

Knox stood up and walked to the door. "Your men can have their workstations back." He left before his friend could ask where he was going. The truth was, he had no idea. He'd already consulted Dr. Mak'en for the day, dinner with Arfilmea wasn't until later, and he couldn't well go and visit Verity.

Maybe he'd take a walk around the ship. It had been an age since he'd done so on his own. Once he became king, he was always escorted by at least one guard—normally Aerue—by his side.

It was like he was a prince again, free to roam his kingdom—though it was much smaller for the time being than he anticipated as a child—without the responsibility of being in charge.

He walked passed dining hall for the humans and glanced inside through the window. Inside, the subjects ate oblivious to his presence because human eyes could not detect most of Eochronian architectural features. All they could see were walls unless something was open. They sat around circular tables with attached benches and a number of his guards surrounded them. It was so different from the grand event gallery it used to be.

But he hadn't had a use for it in a long while. With their guest list always remaining the same, there had been little point in holding parties after the first few centuries aboard the ship.

Until they reached Earth, there weren't many things to celebrate as they navigated the cosmos. And now that they had, the humans needed somewhere to eat that appeared familiar to them compared to the normal teleportation delivery of food from the kitchen to a plate.

As royalty, he was the only one served in the old-fashioned manner of someone physically bringing the food to him. A privilege also enjoyed by anyone who dined with him.

Verity sat at the farthest table from the entrance with her human Captain. They didn't appear to be talking about anything serious, though he would be able to review that on the recordings.

He walked away before anyone could see him spying and continued towards his officers' quarters. The last time he'd traveled there was when his father had given him a tour of the ship. Normally, he only talked to them in his throne room on an individual or small group basis or in the hangar before a larger mission, like when he'd deployed the troop of spies on Earth.

When he entered, the beds were empty. Looking around, there were no personal items anywhere. Most of his soldiers were unmarried, or had lost their spouses when they scrambled to leave their home planet, but he expected to see some record of their loved ones. Especially of those who had been lost.

Then he spotted the thin drawers under each mattress. Very clever on his father's part. It allowed for a private life without distracting from their duties. His grandfather had believed that any soldier should only be married to his duty and his loyalty to the crown, and his father had relaxed those rules substantially.

Personally, Knox saw no reason why either would be in conflict with each other. Especially since no enemy had ever successfully captured one of their kind during past wars. His people were more willing to die rather than be taken alive, and that included spouses who may have otherwise been taken as hostages to use as leverage.

The wives who had survived and were aboard the ship still slept elsewhere to protect them from early morning calls that sometimes happened to keep his men alert and ready for action, even after all these years.

An outsider might ask why Knox hadn't merely repopulated their kind by taking the women of his officers, but he and his father had a suspicion that many were actually his grandfather's children from different affairs. Neither of them could find any evidence of any male children, and he wouldn't have put it past his grandfather to have sent them off to die in the name of his crusade and to protect his lineage.

He loved the man, but there was no denying that he had been a cold and calculating ruler with little room for sentimentality apart from his heirs.

Knox walked past the wives' quarters and continued on to his own. He didn't need to explore the bridge or Aerue and Arfilmea's suite. He'd been there enough times to know it very well. But even though the siblings had separate bedrooms, all three of them were well aware of what occurred during his visits with Arfilmea. Sometimes, he'd take pity on his friend and bring her to his room instead, but he tried not to make that the norm because she tended to treat all spaces as her own and he needed somewhere he could guarantee privacy. His personal dining room had already been compromised by her but so far she'd only entered his bedroom by his invitation. If that ever changed, he had no qualms about revoking her access altogether, at least until they were married.

Doing so might make Aerue like him more, too. Perhaps he should do just that. It wasn't a decision he could make lightly— she was his fiancée, after all—but he would definitely give it more consideration.

He reached his suite and nodded at the sentry stationed there. It wasn't Aerue or Dhaca but the next in line of command.

Inside, he began pacing his bedroom. Dinner wasn't for another couple of hours and he had nothing to do but think. He needed to talk to an engineer about routing surveillance directly into his room as well. Why he hadn't already was an oversight on his part and would need to be addressed immediately. That way, he could keep tabs on the operation without getting in the way of his men doing their jobs, and without the prying eyes of Aerue whose silent judgment was more annoying than anything else.

He opened the door and addressed the guard. "Bring me the chief engineer."

"Yes, Your Majesty."

He closed the door and went back to his study. Now, all he needed to do was wait.

9

VERITY

VERITY'S DOOR opened and a stone-faced Eiz'm stood on the other side, his arms crossed, a pair of manacles gripped in his fist. "Let's go."

He didn't leave enough space for her to try to dart around him. Without another option, she stood up and let him bind her again. Unlike Aerue, Eiz'm tied her wrists in front of her. It made it easier for him to tug her along behind him like an animal on a leash. And he added insult to injury by also attaching an extra pair of shackles around her ankles. All four were connected to the handle he stored at his hip. It was demeaning and so different from Aerue who made her to walk in front of him, but it gave her an opportunity to surreptitiously look around.

As he walked her back to the interrogation room, she kept her eyes and ears open for any clues about what was lying behind the other doors, but silence greeted her behind most except one where she thought she heard a group of voices.

She was pulled forward before she could listen harder.

Lunch had been uneventful and bland, but she now wished she hadn't eaten anything at all. She was already starting to feel physically sick with dread. It used to happen before fighting lessons and even before auditions and performances before her confidence in her abilities grew. But she doubted she would ever feel better about being interrogated by this ass.

He forced her to sit and quickly unlocked the chains before refastening her wrists behind her around the back of the chair. The cold, metal-like material made goosebumps instantly cover her skin. She arched away as much as possible but couldn't escape the cold at her back, and only succeeded in digging the edges further into her scapulas. Why have Eiz'm torture her when the chair was enough on its own?

The alien in question turned his back to her for a moment and she tugged again at her restraints to see if the seat could be leverage and help her break what she couldn't do on her own last night, but nothing happened.

Eiz'm turned back around holding a small syringe. She tried to recoil, but he easily injected her with a clear liquid that warmed her from the inside and made her head spin. What the hell was floating in her bloodstream?

"We're going to try this again," he growled. "And this time, you'll give me answers whether you want to or not. The king said I couldn't use violence with you, but he said nothing about other methods. And I assure you I can be very creative."

That didn't sound good.

"Your name."

It wasn't even phrased as a question and yet she still answered without any hesitation. "Verity Landau."

"Your parents?"

Again, she answered as openly as if she were with a friend rather than being compelled to answer against her will. "Damon and Michelle Landau."

"Any siblings?"

"I'm an only child."

"How old are you?"

"Twenty-two."

The answers flowed out of her before she could catch and prevent them from escaping. Truth serum. She should've known. She knew that different countries around the globe had their own versions, though the use of them were highly kept secrets given the obvious unethical nature of them.

One could assume the highest-ranking senior military officials and those running incredibly sensitive missions were taught to resist similar serums, but she wasn't even sure if her father had undergone that type of training. And there was never a scenario where she would have been exposed to a truth serum either by her own government or by an enemy, so she was as susceptible to it as any stranger who thought the very existence of such an interrogation tool was only a conspiracy to scare others.

Her interrogator nodded. "What is your father's job?"

"He's a Major General in the United States Air Force." God, this was infuriating. To tell herself not to spill her guts and give him what he wanted, but being unable to do anything but just that. She was tempted to close her eyes and pretend it wasn't happening—that she was stronger than a stupid drug, but she couldn't trust Eiz'm, even if he had been forbidden from physically hurting her. He'd already gone behind the king's back once. What was really stopping him from doing it again?

Thanks to the drug in her system, she was already talking so there was no reason he would need to resort to violence during this interrogation, but he had proven himself to be a sadistic bastard in comparison to Knox's amusement with her and Aerue's disinterest courtesy towards her. He was the only one who seemed to actively enjoy the idea of her getting hurt. Especially if he could personally dole out the pain.

He seemed to dislike all humans but she knew on a gut level there was something special about his antagonism towards her that was separate from inter-species animosity. Other than Knox, the other aliens seemed more annoyed by the human presence onboard than anything else, and annoyingly high-handed and conceited in their superior abilities. But Eiz'm specifically had it out for her. She just couldn't figure out if it was because she'd personally done something to piss him off, or if he was displacing his anger at the king onto her. Both seemed equally probable, and maybe it was a combination of the two. It didn't really matter since the end result was the same—him beating her ass, consequences be damned.

Her tormentor's voice broke through her inner monologue. "And what does he do?" From his tone, he was clearly annoyed. Had she spaced out on him speaking? But if she had, she would've expected him to slap her, not merely repeat the question.

Despite her short acquaintance with him, it was clear he was a punch first talk second type of guy. Was he actually following Knox's order to not harm her? She couldn't think of another reason he would show restraint when he was unhappy with her.

If it were a teacher or her father using that tone, she'd already be apologizing, but she had a rule about submitting to assholes: don't ever do it. So, she kept her gaze trained on the door. Giving him attention would only feed his power trip and she didn't feel like looking into his cold eyes and seeing the sadistic gleam there. Her self-control didn't extend to resisting the impulse to answer, so she said, "He strategizes military responses to highly dangerous and secretive threats."

He quickly yanked on the chain hard enough she was worried her shoulders would dislocate. How did this not count as violence? "Be more specific and give me an example."

"A surprise attack from space." He yanked again, demanding a more complete answer, but she bit her lip and forced herself to stay silent.

He pulled a third time, harder than before, and she screamed, unable to contain the verbal expression of her pain. She'd injured herself many times before in dance by overextending during stretching. It wasn't that she was intentionally reckless like at least one instructor had accused her of—something her father had scoffed at when she told him. It was because she genuinely didn't feel the muscle strain before it was too late. And even when one teacher had accidentally done it *to* her while helping her as a child, it hadn't felt like this.

Her anguish only seemed to egg him on, and she that's when she got the idea. She had no idea where the limit of his emotional self control was, but she needed to break it before he broke her. Whether he meant to or not, he'd stop her from spilling the very secrets he was seeking from her. And if he ever figured it out, she'd probably pay for it double the next time she was at his mercy, but she couldn't think about that right now.

"What is your father's plan if beings such as us came to Earth in a large group and demanded obedience?"

Well, if they used a loudspeaker, it would be to give a verbal reply while their countries' military allies cocked their really big guns at the sky and reached out to all other countries to do the same—the fate of humanity was more important than any human war. And all of that would be happening while also relocating the world's most important leaders to a secure underground bunker. Though the goal was also to capture as many alive as possible for further study, the plan was essentially to kill the threat. The research goal wasn't too different from what the aliens had done to her. Minus the fire power. They hadn't needed it, though she had no doubt that given their superior strength and speed that they also had a better arsenal at their disposal.

If she ever got home—*when*, she corrected herself—she'd have to tell her dad that Earth should start openly working together on nuclear weapons rather than pretending no one was doing it. Countries hiding their knowledge from each other was only handicapping themselves if shared resources and research could maybe exponentially boost their progress and chances of survival against these aliens.

Ultimately, it might not matter, if Knox's information about

Earthly weapon systems was anywhere near as thorough as the information he had about food and her. This interrogation aside, he already knew her name before she'd met him. For all she knew, Eiz'm was merely getting her to confirm what they already knew.

But how would they know any of this information to begin with if they didn't have someone on the inside? It was the most likely explanation, but she couldn't fully wrap her head around it. How would they have done it? And how would *no one* at the base know? For it to not even be in the archives? While her dad was on the muscle side of the alien equation, he would read almost anything he could about the unknown enemy to make fighting them easier. What you didn't know you didn't know hurt you more than anything else because you couldn't prepare to defend against it.

And based on how successful the aliens' surprise abduction had been, she was all but certain they were in for a nasty surprise whenever Knox decided to unleash his kind on Earth. He had to eventually because there was no way—or reason—for him to bring all of humanity aboard his ship. Her indefinite stay was an even more demented version of winning a golden ticket, reserved for a select few and not available to the general public.

Her silence couldn't have lasted longer than a few moments, but apparently that was too long for her interrogator because he prompted her again. This time, his tone was even colder and sharper than before. "What is your father's plan in the event of a global disaster?"

God, she wanted to tell him that her father wasn't the one with planning to fight a tsunami or other natural disaster, only for military missions involving extraterrestrials, though he did advise and help execute all emergency plans. In the event of these aliens—or, God forbid, *others*—offering to collaborate on weapons technology rather than fight, her father would be heavily involved in that, too. But the moment it was all about the aliens and nothing about the technology, it was squarely in the space program's purview, and then it was up to the scientists to pass along any pertinent knowledge. But speaking at all, even to correct a misconception, was giving him more information than she wanted to, and would be counter-intuitive to what she was trying to do.

As much as she admired Gandhi and MLK Jr., she'd always thought Malcolm X was more effective, but this passive resistance was proving impressively potent on its own. For the time being at least. She'd eventually have to come up with another plan if she didn't want to suffer permanent brain damage like most pro-athletes. And most of those sports didn't technically allow direct hits to the head whereas that seemed to be Eiz'm's only target.

He lay his hands on the chair's arms and leaned in until their noses were practically touching. If she head-butted him now, it would probably get the job done, but she wanted to know what his next question was. "If you were killed, would your father retaliate?" Eiz'm seemed very tempted to do just that, regardless of what her answer would've been.

Honestly, she couldn't decide. Her father was a very logical man who would never use his rank to get special treatment. On the other hand, she was his only child and she knew he would do anything for her.

Clearly frustrated, he pushed away. Then his fist flew at her, landing a sucker punch to her ribs and knocking the breath out of her.

Motherfucker— that hurt.

She winced, unable to hide the pain and barely able to brace herself before he did the same to the other side. He added two more hits for good measure before she could catch her breath.

"Would your father avenge you? Or would he put the planet before your insignificant life?"

Okay. Now he was just being mean. But she refused to be

baited. She hadn't expected the body hits, though maybe she should've since those could easily be hidden from the king, but if she was right, her plan would start working soon. She just had to keep her mouth shut until it was done.

This time, she saw the hit coming, even as it snapped her head to the side for the second time in two days. The same spot, too. She had to be careful or maybe he'd just snap her neck and find out her father's response himself. But she needed him to do more, or all of this would've been for nothing.

"Wow, orders really mean nothing to you. Why is that? I'd think that to be in your army, you'd have to at least know how to kiss some ass to get this far."

Another blow landed, on the same side he'd just hit. She'd definitely have a bruise, if not a fractured cheek bone soon. Quite frankly, she was shocked she was still conscious. Wasn't it supposed to be three times the charm? He wasn't giving her gentle hits either. She'd seen new trainees fall from a single punch, and she had no doubt that Eiz'm was punching harder than any human could.

"Do you hate all humans or just me?"

"You're special. It's the one thing the king and I agree on."

Huh. For him and Knox to unite on anything was probably a miracle, and for it to be about *her*? She'd definitely have to look into that more once she got out of here and away from this loose cannon. Though with her movements being watched so carefully and no knowledge of how they stored information, that would take some figuring out.

"Is it because I was the only girl taken?" It had been a little weird when she'd only seen men in the captives' mess hall, but given she was used to it on base, she hadn't stopped to consider the implications thought until now. Thinking about it now without the distraction of memorizing new surroundings, it only became stranger. In the grand scheme of an alien abduction, though, especially when they had clearly done reconnaissance on each target beforehand, what were the chances she'd be the only woman taken? Not likely, yet here she was. Alone.

Instead of answering, she was hit again. She smiled. And then she only saw darkness.

Mission accomplished.

10

KNOX

A KNOX on the door was the only warning Knox got before Aerue came in. He looked up and glared at his friend. "You need to ask permission to come in unannounced."

"Who would I ask? I'm the one other people ask, so I already know when you're doing nothing. And I've unfortunately seen you naked before, so don't say that you could have been in the middle of dressing."

It was true. More than that, his friend had unwittingly witnessed him and Arfilmea together more than a few times that Knox had briefly wondered if those instances had been genuine accidents or some twisted voyeurism. He didn't particularly care, but if getting between the siblings eventually forced him to choose Aerue or Arfilmea, he wanted to pick his friend but had to pick his future wife.

His father had warned him that making his best friend his guard and advisor would have some downsides. Being on too familiar a basis with each other was unfortunately one of them. Even so, he wouldn't have picked anyone else if given the chance to go back in time and do it over.

"Why are you here?" he asked.

"Eiz'm interrogated her like you asked, and he used the serum so she was more cooperative and he got some very useful information this time around. You were right about her. She is special in more ways than one."

His friend's words belied his knowledge of Knox's fascination with her, but he hadn't told Aerue how personal it was getting, nor did he plan to. Yes, they'd brought the humans on for a specific purpose, but if anyone knew that he was especially interested in a subject for unscientific reasons, there would be an uproar. Even as though he was the only royal heir of his father, he knew that he had to keep his people happy lest they decide to overthrow him in favor of someone else. It had happened in the past, and was even how his family had come into power on their home planet before colonizing others. He didn't want history repeating itself, especially when he was so close to saving them all.

Aerue had stopped talking, but he could tell there was more. His stoic expression didn't give anything away but his eyes were on the wall instead of him—a telltale sign that his friend was reticent about sharing the rest.

"What else aren't you telling me?" he pressed, though he already suspected he knew. It was Eiz'm, after all, and it was never good news as far as he was concerned.

"He lost his temper and knocked her out when she stopped answering his questions."

Knox saw red. Disobeying a direct order yet again and harming Verity was absolutely unacceptable. He had explicitly told Eiz'm that she was to remain safe and untouched. Only, because she was their best chance and for no other reason.

What was happening that he had to keep repeating himself? First, Arfilmea and now his colonel. They had to reign in their emotions or they would ruin any chance of successfully completing the final phase of his plan. "Get him in the throne room now."

Aerue dipped his head outside and spoke to the guard. Knox heard him walk away.

His friend addressed him again. "From what I understand, she baited him into it."

He wasn't surprised. It sounded exactly like something she would do. But he hoped she now learned that not all Eochrons were as restrained as he was. And it wasn't just because he was schooled in the art of politics and leadership. Aerue was a fighter and showed more restraint than Eiz'm ever had demonstrated. But his father had been the one to promote him to colonel and he couldn't do anything about that without likely causing a mutiny. But he had the power to not promote him, and that's exactly what he'd done. No doubt, that was at least part of the basis for the animosity between them. Even so, orders were orders and if Eiz'm continued this pattern, Knox would be completely in the right to strip him of his rank and military duties. He would even welcome it if it didn't endanger Verity—his plan—in the process.

"She somehow was able to resist the serum's compulsion to talk and became a selective mute."

He'd been picturing her insulting his man until he snapped, but this was unexpectedly restrained of her. "She's very intelligent."

"And seems to have figured out his weak spot."

Eiz'm deserved to have his buttons pushed, but not at the expense of Verity—or the other humans—and by extension everyone on the ship. He wasn't looking forward to seeing him inflict pain on her, but he was perversely anticipating watching Eiz'm lose his composure. It took a lot to break any of his soldiers, and his colonel was normally no exception—aside from their unfortunate ability of getting under each other's skin.

Apparently, Verity was not only a skilled fighter but also skilled in psychological warfare. Trohm hadn't specifically mentioned her being trained in that area, but that wasn't confirmation that she had no experience with it at all. Some people's upbringing was enough to turn a victim into a master in a chain of maladaptive behaviors. His own family was proof of that.

He pulled himself out of his thoughts and saw Aerue still standing there. "I could handle it if you want me to."

"Does he listen to you better?" He was doubtful since Eiz'm's disdain seemed to encompass his personal guard. Guilty by association and bitterness at the perceived nepotism of giving his future brother-in-law such a powerful position. If Eiz'm afforded Aerue more deference, it was still an issue with the chain of command, but it was better than nothing.

"No disrespect, Your Majesty, but he might."

Knox frowned. His friend only used his royal title when things were serious, and he would never fault him for Eiz'm's inappropriate behavior. He tapped his fingers on the desk as he weighed his options. He needed the best outcome, but he also wanted to be the one to reprimand Eiz'm. Not being present at all could also be construed as weakness on his part, being too afraid for the confrontation, and that wouldn't do. "You can come with me and appeal to his better self if I fail to get the message across." If he had one at all.

Aerue held the door open for him and together they walked the short distance to the throne room.

Eiz'm was already there, looking annoyed. That made two of them, because it was absolutely ridiculous to be having this conversation again—even more so that it was within twelve hours since the last time. And it wasn't a failure of short-term memory. It was a deliberate choice Eiz'm made, and these were the consequences.

Knox sat in his throne and looked down at his troublesome subject. Normally, he didn't care for such ceremony and forwent the gesture when speaking to his other soldiers because they already gave him the proper respect. But Eiz'm appeared to need every reminder possible.

Aerue stood in front of his right side, guarding him. His hand rested on the handle of his gun in case the colonel decide to escalate from being inconveniently disobedient to treasonous and attack him.

He didn't bow and instead insolently stared back at him. "Your Majesty," the colonel said tightly, clearly unhappy to be summoned.

He'd brought this upon himself.

"Imagine my surprise when I heard that you incapacitated Miss Landau after I explicitly forbade the use of force against her."

"I had no choice. She was being uncooperative after proving she had valuable information, and you've emphasized the importance of learning all we can about these humans."

It was obvious how much he disagreed. Eiz'm made it no secret that he thought this entire project was a waste of time and that they should merely invade and take Earth's resources for their own. But that solution wouldn't truly solve the problem of their dwindling population. Even if every male paired with every female once, if they didn't do anything, the number of viable mates would eventually dwindle to zero. Inbreeding was common among the Vrulxol, which partially explained their below-average intelligence, and very rare among the Lielneh. The king his ancestor had overthrown was known to have committed incest, but since then, it had been outlawed. And he wasn't about to reverse that declaration.

"That doesn't excuse you disregarding a direct order from your king."

He gave an imperceptible bow, which was somehow more disrespectful than not giving one at all. "You're right," he conceded, but no apology followed.

"If you can't control yourself in interrogation with her, you can leave her to Aerue and focus on the lower prospects. And if you can handle it, even the second-best candidate." Knox saw Aerue's fist tighten around his weapon. It was the only sign of tension or displeasure in his guard's body but he knew what he was going to repeat his speech after their trip to the lab.

"I'm the best interrogator you have," Eiz'm declared. "You might not like how I do it, but I get the results you expect, so I've done my job. Are you sure you want to sideline me so he," Eiz'm nodded his head at Aerue, "someone with less experience in this area of expertise, handling the daughter of the Major General in charge of fighting threats from space? She had started telling me important things before she decided to take on a vow of silence. And if you'd lift this ridiculous ban on force, I could get even more out of her. And isn't that what you're after?"

Interesting that he didn't mention being baited. It was likely a sore point. And he would agree. Being so easily manipulated by a human was definitely a source of embarrassment, and not something he would publicly share if at all possible. But he must have let something slip for another guard to hear and pass onto Aerue for his friend to know about it without seeing the recording. Embarrassment aside, a stronger man would have described the entirety of the situation and owned up to the mistake.

"Yes. It's best for now," Knox said. Honestly, it was the only option until he could trust that Eiz'm wouldn't permanently injure Verity. And he wasn't fully confident that would ever happen. "From now on, you are not to have any interaction with the female subject. Am I clear?"

His colonel didn't answer immediately and the pregnant pause filled the room with enough tension to suffocate them all. "Is that all, Your Majesty?"

He nodded. "You may go."

Eiz'm bowed again, deeper this time, but then he left and turned his back, undercutting the supposed respect he had just shown. It was something he'd never done to Knox's father, but always to him. He sighed. That would likely never change. History had more than proven he would never win with the man, and he could accept that on a personal level but not when it threatened his control as a leader, or those under his protection.

BY THE TIME dinner was ready, Knox was in a foul mood. His chat with Eiz'm had predictably pissed him off and Aerue's subsequent latest attempt to get him to retract his order to begin more intense testing on the human Captain and to offer the same protection to him as he was to Verity.

Instead of responding this time, he'd let his friend have his monologue until Aerue called him out for not saying anything, not even to refute his quasi-accusations.

Aerue was only a few years younger than him and Knox might be king and therefore in charge of his friend, but Aerue managed him more than the other way around. Most of the time, he went along with it because his friend made a good point. Sometimes, it was amusing. Overall, it was white noise because he almost always agreed with his friend at the heart of the matter, though it sometimes took some hashing out to get to that point. But he'd never been so irritated with his advisor for doing his job.

Maybe it was because the advice was now coming from the friend side than the professional side, and not having Aerue back him up felt like a mini-betrayal. It was most probably the words being said. The combination of the two still led to him feeling shitty all the same, and he hated it.

"What's wrong?" Arfilmea asked, pouring him more electrum before refilling her glass.

"It's nothing."

"That can't be true. You've been frowning practically the whole time I've been here."

"I don't want to talk about it, Arfilmea."

"Are things not going well?"

"Everything is fine. Who told you otherwise?" He thought

Aerue had made it clear he didn't want Arfilmea privy to the project's proceedings anymore and that anyone who broke that secrecy would be punished. He wasn't his ancestors who were particularly keen to enact retribution for disobedience but he was was perfectly capable of disciplining his men when necessary.

"No one. I don't know what you said to your men, but no one will tell me anything now." She took a sip and swallowed. "And if that's not the issue, then what's the matter?"

Like he'd tell her.

"Drop it, Arfilmea."

She ate a bite of the dessert. Ever since they were children, she would eat it alongside her main course instead of after. When he and Aerue had asked their fathers for the same treatment, they'd been effectively rebuffed but the future queen had had their fathers wrapped around her slender finger. And once he became king, it wasn't worth enforcing the rule that all his dinner guests wait to move on until he was done. She was the exception, and she enjoyed that privilege with the attitude that it was inevitable. She moved through life with that assumption and he couldn't blame her given she had rarely been proven wrong.

They ate in silence for a few moments. He kept his eyes on his plate and ignored the fact that she was practically boring a hole into him with her pensive stare. As much as he and Aerue teased her for being frivolous, she was incredibly intelligent. And having that sharp mind focused on him made him want to shift in his chair like a child caught after doing something wrong.

"Stop," he said.

"But I didn't say anything."

"You were thinking."

"Well, yes. Contrary to popular belief, I do that from time to time. You're just unhappy because I'm going to figure out your secret."

Unlikely. But if he said that out loud, it would only challenge her and strengthen her resolve.

He shrugged.

She pointed her knife at him. "It has to be her."

Was he really that easy to read? Or was it just that way to the two people who knew him best? Even so, he needed to get better at concealing his feelings fast.

"If you're done," he glanced down at her empty dessert plate, "you can leave."

"See? I'm right. You never kick me out without having fun first."

"This project is taking a lot out of me." Truth. "I'm tired." Partial lie. "I'm not in the mood." Also true. "Maybe we should take a break before the wedding."

Now, it was her turn to frown. She stood and walked over to him, resting a hand on his shoulder. "Are you sure?" she asked softly, her hand drifting down to stroke his chest. "We have fun, don't we?"

Her not wanting to be a mother was only a preference. She wasn't at risk of getting pregnant by accident. Unlike humans, his kind were long-able to voluntarily control fertile periods.

"Yes," he said.

Her hand dropped. "Okay, then." He watched her walk to the door. "I'll see you another time," she said. It was both a question and a promise.

"Goodnight," he said.

She left without another word.

He stared at his half-eaten meal and sighed. He summoned the chef's assistant to clear the dinnerware. His chef would likely want to know what went wrong given he always finished his food, but that would be a conversation for tomorrow.

He barely finished pulling off his clothes before he fell into bed. The days appeared to be getting longer, and the journey to his end goal was proving more arduous than expected. He couldn't wait until his project was finished, and then he'd be able to leave this ship for the first time in many millennia. That day would be a celebration larger than any he'd ever witnessed, and then perhaps the others in his life would fall in line and his life would be perfect. He could dream and, after restlessly pacing his room and staring at the ceiling for too long, that's exactly what he did.

11

VERITY

VERITY WAS ALREADY EATING, carefully moving her jaw that was still sore, when Ben came into the mess hall. Last night, she had planned on waiting for him, but she woke up with such bad hunger pangs that she hadn't experienced outside of final exams in a long time. Which was strange given how filling the food felt after the meals. Only another reason to be suspicious of it. The fact still remained that it was the only option other than starving to death, and that clearly wasn't going to work if her caving this morning was any indication.

He sat down and raised a singular, judgmental eyebrow but started eating too. Her shoulders dropped as the anxiety of him going on a hunger strike abated.

He scowled.

Something was wrong but she didn't know what. Her shoulders immediately rose again. A stress response she'd spent years trying to get rid of at the behest of fight and dance instructors alike. At this point, she'd given up on the idea of not having the issue, but at least she now made a more conscious, daily effort to readjust whenever she felt it happen.

"What happened?" he asked. "If the king did that to you, I'll kill him."

She touched the side of her face. How had she forgotten about it already? Then she saw the guards all stand at attention. She hissed, "Are you crazy? Don't make threats like that, Ben. They'll kill you."

"I thought you said we were safe from that."

"Don't be be a smart-ass." How many times had he told her the same thing after mouthing off to a new recruit who hadn't yet understood her place among the STFs? "I don't think that extends to you trying to assassinate their leader."

"Didn't you try that on our first night here?"

She glared, but he didn't seem bothered. Not that she expected him to. His glare had always been more effective than hers, and it was annoying that it worked on her but not vice versa.

"Leave it alone, Ben. I'm begging you." If his self-preservation wasn't kicking in to silence him, and she couldn't intimidate him into it, maybe he'd do it for her as a favor. "It's not worth getting upset about. It happened. It's over. There's nothing you or he can do about it."

"What the hell does that mean? He's the king, isn't he?"

"There's an order that I'm not supposed to be harmed, but clearly," she gestured to the swollen side of her face, "the interrogator has gone rogue and didn't listen." There was no reason for Ben to know about her ribs. He'd likely become murderous and get himself killed. "Though, in this case, I did provoke him."

Incredulous understanding dawned in his eyes. "On purpose?"

"The bastard injected me with truth serum. It was the only way I could think of to make me stop talking. And instead of the lecture I know you're about to give, if you have any other suggestions, now would be a great time to tell me. I'm probably going to be interrogated again later today, and I'd prefer not having to get my lights punched out again."

Verity snuck a glance at the thirteen guards. They were pretending not to listen but she knew better. She still asked her question, though because whatever Ben was about to answer would be knowledge their captors already had. "So, what did you tell them?"

"Whatever he asked me until I figured out why I couldn't lie. He got as far as my dad's position before I forced myself to stay quiet and switched tactics."

"Did you divulge any specifics?"

She shook her head and ate another bite. If she didn't think about the texture, it was fine. Which part of the reason why she was eating like the STFs she grew up around rather than the way her mother had taught her before she died and her father enforced during meals at home. Scarfing the food down as fast as humanly possible so the nutritional value was gained without suffering through any bad tastes that might be mixed in. The Meals Ready to Eat they had during field training wasn't exactly Michelin star-quality, and neither was the food here.

He sighed. "That's a relief at least." He looked down at his food before looking back up at her, his brow furrowed in confusion. "How did you resist it at all?"

"I have no idea." Just another thing she didn't understand. And it had been surprisingly easy in comparison to unsuccessfully actively lying. She hadn't even been able to give bare bone answers while omitting more important details. Telling Eiz'm her father was a general would have been bad enough but then divulging his specialty and more had been so much worse. Why couldn't she have just said, *He does his job*, when asked what he did. It wouldn't have been a lie and it would've pissed Eiz'm off for sure, but it also maybe wouldn't have required her to go to such extreme measures.

The door opened and Ben tensed beside her. Verity didn't have to look to know that Aerue had come to collect her again. It was clear after her special breakfast yesterday that Knox had expected it to become routine. But there was no way in hell that she was going to entertain the king today. She might be his prisoner and her life was in his hands, but she wasn't a dog doing tricks for food.

"No," she said before he even reached her.

He came to a stop in front of her, a scowl slashed across his face. "It's not a request." He didn't seem happy about the king's decision, but she didn't have any hope she could convince him to go against Knox's choice.

"And I told you no."

He took another step forward and she suddenly saw Ben's back as he stepped in front of her, shielding her from the king's right hand man. She was equally flattered and annoyed. While she appreciated the gesture, she didn't need anyone to protect her. And Eiz'm had proved to be the exception when it came to following Knox's directive to treat her with kid gloves. Or, at the very least, not violent. She still couldn't say that the guards chaining her up tightly was gentle.

Verity had no doubt that Aerue would do whatever he needed to in order to get her to the king's breakfast but she didn't see him starting a violent altercation in the midst of the other humans. If they revolted, the guards would still overpower them, but she doubted Knox wanted any instances of united rebellion among the prisoners. It would plant the idea, and that was sometimes the most dangerous aspect because ideas were almost impossible to kill.

"If she doesn't want to go, she's not going," Ben growled.

She touched Ben's arm. His muscle tensed and spared a quick glance at her before returning his attention back to the alien intent on taking her away. At least this time it wasn't another violent abduction. She stepped out sideways from behind him, so she could see both men.

"Guys," she said, trying to get their attention off each other. The less time they spent thinking about how to take the other down, the better it would turn out for everyone. "Take it easy. Fighting each other isn't going to change my mind."

Aerue ignored her and kept advancing until he stood chest to chest with Ben.

Verity sighed. Words weren't working. She wedged herself between them. Aerue turned his attention back to her, but Ben didn't take his attention off the alien.

"You can tell Knox that if he wants to see me again, he needs to control his people."

The guard finally looked at her again, his eyes flashing with incredulity. She couldn't think of why.

"It's already been handled," he answered. "Now, come with me, Miss Landau. You've already kept the king waiting long enough. He's not known for his patience."

"I never guaranteed I'd go. And I'll believe it when I see it. Forgive me if I don't believe you. What's to say Eiz'm won't do it again?"

"He will not be talking to you again."

She pointed to her face. "You call this talking?"

He didn't even flinch, and she fought the urge to slap him. The guards filling the room would likely take her down and accidentally hurt her even if they were trying to avoid doing so.

"From now on, I am responsible for you. Is that a satisfactory answer for you?"

She held his gaze until he finally backed down.

"Very well. I'll see you later." He didn't say it threateningly, but a shiver ran up her spine at the knowledge that this enigma of a person would be interrogating her from now on. She couldn't read him to save her life and that was an issue.

They watched him leave and it wasn't until the door sealed behind him that she and Ben sat back down.

"So," he said, "you're working your way up the power structure very easily. You refused to cooperate with one, and now you have to deal with someone even more important."

If she didn't know Ben better, she'd think he was making a perverse comparison to the sexist and frustratingly persistent stereotype that women had to sleep their way to the top.

"I guess so," she muttered. Though she'd met the very top her first night on the ship. It wasn't like she'd had to go through Aerue to meet him. It had just happened at his command.

"Eiz'm's clearly an enforcer, but I can't figure out his rank."

"Definitely military, though I can't quite tell his rank either. Especially if he's acting inappropriately for his position."

"Aerue," she indicated the door when Ben gave her a blank look, "is King Knox's right hand."

"Is he a weakling?"

"Who? Aerue?" Had Ben experienced the last few minutes entirely different than she had? "No. He's the one who stopped me from attacking Knox the first night without breaking a sweat. He might be able to give you a run for your money."

"If you hadn't intervened, you might had the chance to test your hypothesis. But I meant the king." He paused. "And you use their first names?"

"Why wouldn't I? You don't expect me to use some ridiculous title to avoid it? We're not living in a children's book where saying a name is a crime or a way enemies can track you." Of course, governments could do something similar if they were already keeping tabs on certain keywords, but it wasn't much of an issue otherwise.

"That's not it, though you have to know that they're going to take notice if you insist on calling all of them by name. Especially their king.

Maybe *that* was why Aerue had been surprised earlier. She doubted many others, if anyone, called Knox by his name.

"I just wouldn't have thought he would share anything personal with you. You must've made quite the impression on him."

What the hell was he going on about? "It's not like he told me during an intense heart to heart. It was a simple, overdue intro-duction." She was still a little surprised that he'd leveled the playing field of putting them on a first-name basis given how difficult he'd been during their first meeting. But he still wasn't an open book by a long shot. He'd definitely buried the lead on him being the king. "What's your point?" She didn't bother apolo-gizing for her snapping. He was being annoyingly and uncharac-teristically cagey. It was pissing her off.

One of the things she loved about being friends with Ben was that there was no bullshit between them. Or, there never had been, but one forced breakfast date with an alien king and now Ben couldn't spit out whatever he seemed to be choking on. Sure, he was still being straightforward about certain things, but he was holding back and talking in circles more than she'd ever known him to.

"If he's always having other people doing his dirty work and didn't even try to defend himself against you, I'm wondering if he even could, assuming you got past his right hand, as you said."

She didn't miss his refusal of using any of their names. It probably kept them as a kind of faceless enemy and easier to attack brutally. It was something taught to everyone in the United States military, with the exception of the worst of the worst who were specifically identified as an individual, but she wasn't a soldier. And she was a people person more than anything, and that required meant she needed to see people as individuals to better read them and adjust her behavior. It was something she'd always done, not just with their alien captors, and it was a method that hadn't failed her yet.

"I don't know," she finally answered. "Like I said, I've never fought him. But he didn't seem concerned at all when I went for him so he's either completely confident in Aerue's ability to protect him, or he knows that he could defend himself fine if all else failed."

Ben inclined his head, taking in the information. "Well, we know he has a soft spot for you,"

Did they really know that? Right now, it was just a hunch. And Knox wanting her alive and not bruised didn't strike her as a particularly tender expression from him but maybe she was just extra cynical having met him and was letting her personal feelings cloud her judgment.

Even with Ben's overprotective streak, he was technically more objective than her on Knox's character because he hadn't met the king yet. He'd seen the concrete outcomes of his actions, and nothing else.

"I think you should take him up on his invitation the next time one comes around."

She coughed, practically choking on the mush they'd been given for breakfast. "You can't be serious. You just backed me up when I didn't want to go."

Ben lowered his voice to barely above a whisper. "He might let something slip."

"I've already tried," she muttered. "He's just as tight-lipped as me, if you ignore this morning, of course. And there's no chance in hell I could get close enough to him to give him some truth serum if I could manage to grab that."

"I'm just saying you should try again."

"How do you even know he'll ask me again after I rebuffed him?"

"Who can resist you?"

She almost laughed before she realized he was serious. Verity swallowed. Was this him admitting he felt some attraction toward her, too, or was this just the strategy?

He was still waiting for her answer to the plan.

She rolled her eyes and leaned forward, bringing their faces closer together. "Fine. I'll do it." But she wasn't looking forward to it.

"Good. And you'll keep me updated."

"I'm not the one in the military, Ben, so drop the in-charge act. You don't give me orders. The only ones who can do that here are the assholes who took us. If I don't listen to them, and my life is in their hands, I'm not going to listen to you on this."

He raised an imperious eyebrow. If he was surprised by her outburst, he didn't say it. Nor did he apologize.

She clearly wasn't going to win this fight, so Verity changed the subject. They had more important things to deal with but she could still feel the band of anger around her chest. "Where are they keeping you?"

"Twenty steps side if you turn right out of here. Can you get some paper?"

"I'm half that distance past you on the same side. I pass your room every day." That meant they could secretly communicate with each other. That is, if she could get a writing implement. She looked up at him. "How much do you remember Major Davies' classes?"

"Pretty well. You?" He smiled, a challenge in his tone.

She smiled smugly. "Very well."

12

KNOX

KNOX STARED at the door and took long draw from his drink. He was too anxious to handle solid food, but he continued picking at it to keep up appearances. If Aerue noticed, he'd be getting a visit from Dr. Mak'en, not just the chef. He didn't have patience for either. Both of them had jobs to do and diverting their attention to him was unnecessary and counterproductive. But convincing his friend he was fine would be an impossible task, so he took another bite of food and washed it down with more morning nectar. It would get him through the day with the daily requirements of nutrition. Everything else was for taste and unfortunately wasted on him this morning.

"What are you thinking about?"

He turned his attention back to his companions. Arfilmea was regarding him with the same probing gaze as last night.

"I was expecting your human to be here."

So had he. Once again, his betrothed had invited herself to breakfast but this time the guest he *had* invited failed to appear. And he still didn't know why. He turned his attention to Aerue who sat on his other side.

His friend hadn't given him an answer when he returned empty-handed and had immediately started eating.

"Why did she refuse?" he asked.

He had planned to talk to Aerue after Arfilmea had left to give them privacy and keep her in the dark about his derailed plan. But his friend's reticence at sharing made him even more restless to know why he was in his current situation. As a king, he should be in control of his life, but Verity's arrival had upended any command he had over Eiz'm, Arfilmea, and his own thoughts and feelings. The longer he was forced to wait, the worse her influence grew. Like a parasite burrowing under his skin. If he didn't address it soon, no one would be happy. Least of all himself. Because while she and her kind was fascinating, her role had to remain a small, limited one. His obsession with her was growing, as was his need for the project's completion. Both would culminate in him getting her out of his system and eventually his life, once she had played her part.

"She said that if you want to see her again, you need to, and I quote *control your people*. She didn't care that I told her that it was already done since I'd be interrogating her from now on."

He should have expected a cutting remark, but she certainly didn't mince words.

"Did you explain to her that the circumstances have changed?"

"I did. She still refused."

Why was she being so stubborn when she clearly got a better meal eating with them than with all the other humans?

"I would've insisted but her Captain got involved. I made an executive decision because I thought it best not to—" he glanced at his sister and clearly said something different than what he'd originally intended to, "start a riot. I'm sure you agree it was the right choice."

Now it all made sense. She hadn't just rejected him, but also chosen her human companion over him. The man just kept getting in the way, didn't he? Eventually, their tie would have to be severed, but he knew doing so now would only antagonize her and as amusing as it was to verbally spar with her, he couldn't actually have her hate him. And it seemed she was already half way there without him actively doing anything since she boarded the ship.

Perhaps he needed to have a talk with this man and learn what he could from him about Verity. He might be tightlipped about his role in the government, though not nearly as successfully as Verity, but he surely he'd be more willing to share about their friendship. It was an innocuous enough topic that it should be easy to get answers about her.

"So, how's the project going?" Arfilmea asked. Was her interest due to him not answering her before or because she suspected how much a particular human was occupying his mind?

Telling her a general status update wasn't too much to ask. If she was going to eventually become a leader of their people, she deserved to have an inkling of their future as a species. He hadn't wanted to tell her at the start because her questions would be constant and distracting—she was proving him right on that account—but at this point, giving in to her might be the only way to get a reprieve.

"Well. There are some candidates who may be ready soon, though there's no guarantee on the timing." Or that it would work at all. He pushed the thought out of his mind. It would work. They had eighteen chances of yielding success, and two of them had a higher probability than the others. There was nothing to indicate that the lower range would fail altogether, so he could technically afford to be even more optimistic. Realistically, he had to acknowledge all of them might not survive, but enough would to get the job done, and once the process had been perfected, it could be applied to a larger sample group until they could unleash it on the whole planet.

"Oh? Are there any handsome ones in the group?"

He turned to Aerue, who'd seen all the subjects up close whereas he'd personally only seen Verity. Forcing her brother to field the question was probably cruel but he wasn't about to presume to know what Arfilmea looked for in men. Getting married was already guaranteed to change the dynamic between them to some degree, and helping her choose future partners was taking things too far.

His friend rolled his eyes. "Yes, sister. You would consider some of them as such, though I wouldn't get your hopes up."

"There's one in particular you might like." If he could pair the human Captain off with Arfilmea, that would solve more than one of his problems. Once Arfilmea became his queen and given birth to an heir and a spare, they could live independent lives while she amused herself with the human Captain and he would do the same Verity. But he was getting ahead of himself.

"Really?" she asked. "Maybe this idea of yours isn't so crazy after all. Though they are still part human." She wrinkled her nose.

"Thank you so much for your vote of confidence," he said. "Remember, you said you'd participate. You don't like Eiz'm or any of the others, and if we're being totally honest, you don't like me in that way either."

She sniffed. "But we have to get married. Our people need a queen, and you need an heir."

As if he needed the reminder.

She sounded slightly upset though he couldn't understand why. Neither of them had ever romanticized their planned union. Even when she used to torture him with wedding-planning talk, it was more about her fantasy of having a perfect day and party where she was the center of attention than celebrating was, years of friendship aside, an essentially transactional alliance.

"What we really need is to rebuild our population," he corrected. "I'm not going to force you to exclusively be with me for the rest of our lives to do that." She always got bored within a few months, and he didn't want her to ever resent him for taking away more freedoms than he had to with their arrangement. And even if they were happy together, multiple millennial always took its toll on a relationship with ups and downs along the way. Best not to start off on a bad note.

Her mouth dropped open, and he saw panic enter her lapis eyes. "You're considering cancelling the wedding?"

"That's not what I said. Why would you even say that?" Her mind had jumped rather quickly to that alarming conclusion. Was he wrong in assuming she'd been looking forward to becoming his queen? Just yesterday, they had talked about post-poning having children—at her request, no less—and now she wanted to call off what was essentially her stake in the deal. The only thing that had happened between them since then was him turning down her advances after dinner. "If this is about last night—"

Aerue cleared his throat and Knox cut himself off. But that had to be it because he and Arfilmea had been on the same page when he'd left the library, and he'd been forced to compromise on when they'd start building his lineage.

"What am I supposed to think? You've postponed the wedding until this project is over. And you've put a pause on us." Her brother winced, but she continued without stopping to draw breath. "If I didn't know any better, I'd say you were avoiding me. And you're spending all your free time thinking about or checking in on the humans. But that's not going to give you what you need. Unless—You can't be serious. *That's* the point of it all, isn't it? You think she'll let you get close enough to do that?"

"Don't be crass," he snapped.

"Even worse, you'd be diluting our gene pool even further. Your heir needs to be someone all of us can support. You know there are people who will never bow to a hybrid."

There were some who already never bowed to him. "Do you

count yourself among them?" If she wasn't going to be support-ive, perhaps he needed to find someone else to be his queen. Though that would require more time and research, which would only serve to legitimize the concerns some of his kind already had about the project.

"Of course not!" She looked affronted, but her reaction was a little too exaggerated. What was she playing at?

"My plans for the humans are none of your concern at the moment. And we're working on addressing that issue," he snapped. He pushed back from the table and stood.

"Where are you going?"

Why wouldn't she just leave him alone? Before the humans had come aboard, she hadn't hung around him this much since they were children.

"Leave him be, Arfilmea. You've done enough damage for one morning, don't you think?"

He left without answering, making his way to the labora-tory. Maybe they could give him the piece of mind he so desperately needed right now. Aerue followed him out, leaving Arfilmea alone at the table. He didn't look back to check on her.

Once outside, he turned to Aerue. "I know she's your sister, but I don't want her barging into my private meals anymore. And I want the Captain observed more closely from now on. Espe-cially if he's with Miss Landau."

"We could just separate them during mealtimes, even if she doesn't eat with—" he cut himself off. A wise choice on his part.

"No. They speak openly with each other. We can't let them know we understand them. Trohm has been keeping me informed of their conversations." He paused. "And I want her to join me for dinner." He was still jealous of her company, and if he was going to let her stay with her friend for meals at all, he deserved something out of the deal. "Do whatever you need to for her to agree but don't—"

Aerue waved him off. "Harm her. Yes, I know. You've made yourself very clear on that front. I promise I won't harm her."

"Good." He was a little scared how far he would go to protect Verity, and what he would do to anyone who dared defy him and hurt her.

"You know my sister means well, don't you?"

"I'm not about to accuse her of treason," he said. "But I had no idea she felt this way about what I was doing. I was under the impression that she liked it better than you. You don't need to lie," he added before his friend could protest. "I know you were never a fan of it from the start. But you've supported me all the same, and I appreciate it."

Aerue's semi-permanent scowl disappeared. "Of course," he replied. "You're not only my king but also my friend. If I thought it was a disastrous mistake, I also would have told you before it got this far. I am still skeptical, but I must admit there is a chance that this outlandish scheme works."

"Maybe you'll find someone to occupy your time with, too."

"Impossible. I don't know why you keep trying to pair me off with someone. I'm not interested, and even if I were, I wouldn't have the time for anyone else in my life. I spend all my time making sure you don't get into too much trouble. Maybe if you took a break every so often it could work."

"So, you've thought about it?"

"It's a purely hypothetical thought experiment. Like I said, I'm not interested in anyone in that way. And I mean *anyone*."

Knox smiled. "Alright. I won't ask again in the future."

"I can't believe it took me turning down humans for you to finally get to this point. I've been telling you this for years."

Well, when he put it like that... "I'm sorry. I should have listened to you when you first told me. I've been a bad friend."

"Don't be melodramatic. And the most important thing is you finally understand."

"Well, I don't know if I'd go that far. I can't empathize with your situation, but I can accept that's part of who you are."

"Yes, I know it would be impossible for you to be in my position on this matter. And that's all I've wanted," Aerue said. "Now, please change the subject."

"What do you want to talk about?" He would like to ask about how security had been regarding the humans, but delving back into project details after the breakfast discussion didn't seem wise. He was about to have a conversation with Dr. Mak'en so there was no reason to subject Aerue to it.

"You're not eating." It wasn't a question, and both an accusation and condemnation simultaneously.

Clearly, he hadn't done a well enough job at disguising the fact from him.

"Is something wrong?"

"Just overthinking things."

"Ah."

He glanced sideways at his friend. "What does that mean?"

"Sometimes I wonder if you think at all."

"Weren't you just praising me for thinking up my project?"

"Praise? You're self-aggrandizing. And this endeavor aside, you let your emotions guide you more than you should."

There was no mistaking his meaning.

He didn't deign to give a response. He walked faster until they reached the laboratory and he entered before Eiz'm could announce him. His visits were routine enough that the scientists likely were expecting him. Even if they weren't, they could recover quickly.

Sure enough, they rose from their seats at the sound of his entrance, turned to face him and bowed. It wasn't quite in unison, but it was very close.

"Dr. Mak'en," he said. "Status report?"

"You realize, Your Majesty, that these things take time, and your regular visits only slow our progress?"

He stared at her and saw the other junior scientists and assistants quickly turned back to their work, trying to shrink into the background. Wise choice on their part.

"I'm going to pretend you didn't just say that and give you the opportunity to give me the update I asked for."

She led him over to a table showcasing the data. "The minimum has been raised, but the ones in the middle haven't seen as much improvement. And before you ask, the second best also hasn't changed enough to mention."

"You just did."

"I'm being thorough," she said. "Did you have any specific questions for me?"

He shook his head.

"Very well. If you think of anything else, you'll let me know. But knowing in advance is always preferable." The unspoken chastisement reminded him of how his mother would react to his childhood mischief. "That way I can prepare a presentation for your next visit."

"I'll see what I can do. Thank you for entertaining my curiosity. I'll let you get back to work." He turned and left.

Aerue was smiling.

"What?"

"She essentially told you to get out of the way. Maybe now you'll finally take a break from micromanaging them."

"Don't you have something better to do than hammer this point? Go review the surveillance."

"What will you do, then?"

Find Arfilmea and patch things up. She was still a close friend and his fiancée.

13

VERITY

VERITY TOOK A DEEP BREATH, trying to release the knot in her stomach. She followed the guard out of her room, but they weren't heading towards the cafeteria for lunch. It was too early for that. But that wasn't the first deviation of what she was used to today. Things had been wrong since breakfast ended, when she'd been escorted back to her room.

Aerue had asked her yet again to join the king, but this time, when she'd turned down the request, he hadn't pushed as hard as last time. It seemed every time she had refused over the past few weeks, the more the guard liked her. Strange.

The daily schedule she'd grown accustomed to during her time on the ship—almost two weeks now—was simple. Breakfast was immediately followed by a stress test and a shower. Then lunch happened, and afterward she was interrogated. Lastly, she was given time to recover in her room until dinner. Three meals a day with thirteen guards and eighteen prisoners including her and Ben.

But *today*, she had been promptly brought to the interrogation room for a session with Aerue immediately after breakfast, forgoing the stress test altogether. She wasn't sure if it was better or worse to have him so early in the day.

She'd been forced to talk more about her regular schedule at home on the base, and that of the STFs she knew. Luckily, she'd stopped privy to most of the details since she started college at UNLV. She'd been able to keep that part a secret because even though it had nothing to do with her father or the United States military, it was personal information she didn't need these aliens knowing. One *royal* pain-in-the-ass, especially. Eiz'm had only seemed to care about her father, and though Aerue was apparently interested in a larger scope of details, her lie of omissions went largely unnoticed.

The free time she'd been unexpectedly granted after breakfast was more an opportunity for her to torture herself about what was happening than an extra opportunity to relax without being obviously scrutinized by her captors. She was still fully aware that there were probably cameras in her room, but she'd adjusted to living her life normally in her personal space. Of course, it was still worlds apart from what she'd be doing at home. For one, she'd have her phone and laptop and would be spending her free time with friends, practicing moves, or falling down an online rabbit hole. The last rarely happened thanks to her father's strict rule about it while she was growing up but it still happened every so often.

She followed the guard into a new room that appeared just like the one she normally took her stress tests in, but the ceiling was lower and there was no machine waiting for her. And instead of the normal singular adhesive applied over her heart, the guard placed two of them on her chest, and two of them on her back. He left without a word. It seemed Aerue was the only guard who ever talked to her beyond telling her it was time to go somewhere. Maybe they'd been instructed not to engage with her. And though Aerue was chatty in comparison to those under his command, his speaking to her was always predicated on him relaying messages from the king. It wasn't as if he wanted to make conversation. She still couldn't get him to talk to her of his own volition.

She walked around the perimeter of the room, searching for any hidden openings. As expected, she couldn't find any. It was just large enough that she wasn't merely pacing back and forth.

And then water started filling the room. It wasn't coming out of the ceiling like the shower, but was rapidly rising out of the floor. Looking down, she couldn't distinguish any source of the water.

It was already at her ankles, and was just brushing the hem of her pants. But it didn't stop there and continued its progress. What was happening? She backed up until she met the wall. No escape. What the hell? Were they trying to drown her?

She glanced around the room again, searching for a camera. Unable to find one, she just glared at the ceiling and then the far wall for good measure. Hopefully, someone would see that on the recording. If she died, at least they'd have an inkling of how monumentally she pissed she was in her final moments.

The level reached her neck. She barely hovered off the ground, buoyed by the very thing that would likely kill her. She started treading water to keep her head above water. She had always thought the expression was trite, but literally experiencing it was so much worse. And the worst part was she wouldn't be able to hold out forever. The flooding showed no sign of stopping and she'd eventually be underwater. Her clothes were now thoroughly soaked and weighed her down, making everything more difficult.

She closed her eyes and forced herself not to think about the consequences of what she was about to do. Without hesitation, she shucked off the pants and pulled off the top. Instantly, she felt lighter, but it wasn't enough.

She took a gulp of air just in time before all the space above the surface was obliterated. She might not have fully completed scuba diving training but she still had an impressive time when it came to holding her breath. She just hoped whatever sick game they were playing with her ended before she started drowning for real.

She opened her eyes and was relieved it wasn't chlorinated or irritating in some other way. She doubted the aliens used the same chemicals on Earth. She swam down to the floor, searching yet again for an opening. She could still feel water coming in which meant it also had to be leaving. She ran her fingers over the floor and felt tiny jets. But where was it draining? She looked up at the sides of the room and did the same thing. This time, she felt her finger get sucked in by a vacuum.

She slapped the wall in frustration. Yes, she'd found the water's exit point but it was too small for her to fit through. She felt her lungs start to burn and began exhaling as slowly as possible. Once she ran out of air, it would be *the end*. And she wasn't ready to die yet.

At least she could be grateful not to have a painful piercing sensation in her ears. The room wasn't big enough for the depth to exert an unbearable amount of force, even at the bottom where she was. She'd been in pools with more severe deep ends than this.

Verity turned over and kicked until she was lying on the ground. She watched the bubbles rise from her mouth and nose up to the ceiling. Her lungs were burning and everything in her body was trying to force her to take a breath but she knew that inhaling would only flood them with water. Either way, she was going to die, so why make it more painful for herself? When the air stopped, she crossed her arms over her chest as if she were in a casket. Was she being dramatic? A little. But given this was her watery *grave*—why not?

She closed her eyes, gave one final exhale, and waited for the end to come.

She woke up lying in a room she'd never seen before, lying on a cold table. Was she dead? Brought back to life? Who knew the extent of these aliens' technology? Maybe it was easy for them to be Frankenstein while humanity still struggled to solve the problem of bringing people back to life.

Personally, as much as she missed loved ones who had died, she thought the dead should stay that way. Every book and movie about it happening successfully inevitably led to disaster, whether it be possessed corpses, zombies, and vampires—who were essentially undead, super-powered murderers. And if they'd brought her back to life, their plan was probably even more sinister than she initially thought. Were they able to control her now that they'd resurrected her?

She touched her chest, expecting to find the sensors still there, but they were gone. And she was once again wearing a pair of clothes. When had that happened?

"Can you hear me?"

She turned her head and saw a young man wearing a plain coat. It was the first outfit that didn't match the guards' aside from Knox's wardrobe. Even Eiz'm and Aerue only had variations of the standard uniform.

"Yes," she said. She sat up and felt a wave of dizziness hit her. Not good.

"You should lie back down. You've been through an ordeal."

Orchestrated by you, or your boss, she thought. "I'll be fine," she said. And it was the truth. She could already feel the disorienting sensation disappearing.

"All the same, I need you to stay here for a bit longer. I need to monitor you more."

"Wasn't that what you were doing while I was drowning?"

He didn't react to her accusation aside from blandly stating, "This is different."

She looked down at her body again. She didn't see anything attached to her. How were they observing her without any devices? She might not know how the stickers worked, but they were obviously sensors of some kind. She had no idea what information they reported to her alien captors, but she assumed they needed *something* to go off.

The man circled her and she did her best to turn her head to keep him in her sight. Just as she was about to completely turn around, he reached out and touched the base of her neck.

She froze.

"Please look straight ahead, I have to inspect the back of your head."

If this was anything like that famous dystopian sci-fi film series, she was in trouble. Maybe she wasn't the creature in a horror film but a minion in a technological nightmare.

"What are you doing?"

He didn't respond.

Verity rolled her eyes. She should have known better.

True to his word, he walked back into her view.

"Well?" she asked. "Did I pass?"

"That wasn't a test."

He was actually making conversation? She wasn't about to waste the opportunity to get whatever information she could. Verity kept talking. "But the water thing was."

To her surprise, he nodded. "If you'd like to, you can lie back down and relax."

He expected her to *relax*?

Her disbelief must have been apparent because he continued, "If you're hungry, someone will take you the cafeteria for lunch."

She was. But she also felt like sleeping for a week. She wasn't even positive she could stomach solid food at the moment. "And if I'm not?"

"Then you will be returned to your room until dinnertime."

Lovely. "Lunch," she said, before the choice could be made for her. At the very least, she'd get to see Ben there.

. . .

BEN WASN'T there when she sat down. She sat, staring at the door as her handlers got her food for her. Then she ate slowly, waiting for him to arrive. The moment she stopped eating, she'd be whisked away to her room and she didn't want to be alone again just yet.

For once, the food was actually half-way decent in texture. It still wasn't as familiar as the food she had when she dined with Knox, but it was better than the mush they'd been getting since being forced onto the ship. It seemed a little counterintuitive, though. Improving the food situation in the cafeteria only lowered this chances. Maybe another prisoner had complained? Though why they would change course for that didn't make much sense either.

She knew the world didn't revolve around her but the king seemed almost hellbent at times to get her company. He was conspicuously absent from her life during the past few meals. No invitations or mandatory summonings had been issued. It was both relieving and worrying that he seemed to have lost interest in her.

There weren't clocks anywhere and she only saw windows when she was with Knox but from what she could tell. She'd been counting the *days* by meals but time was also a blended, continuous spectrum that was slowly numbing her mind. The only thing keeping her sharp was her determination to get out of this floating hell hole.

She was almost done when Ben finally walked in. His hair was wet, and he looked more pissed than ever seen him. She stood up to greet him.

He didn't say anything but sat down silently, banging the table with his fists and jostling it as he situated himself on the attached bench. It was like she was back in elementary school—when the teachers hadn't trusted the kids not to play with or destroy the chairs. Though their captors were more likely worried about a free-standing chair's potential as a weapon than whether or not it was stable enough to be sat on.

"What happened to you?" she asked.

"I almost drowned. You?"

She sat up straighter. "Same." Was it happening to everyone or just the two of them? Over the last few days, she'd noticed most of the guards—even those who hadn't escorted them into the cafeteria—spent more of their attention on the two of them than any of the other prisoners.

"If they were going to torture us in a new way, you'd think they'd do a better job at it. You're not supposed to accidentally *kill* the person before they can give you an answer."

A guard put food down in front of Ben. Before the alien had returned to his post by the wall, Ben continued, "Waterboarding would've been more effective."

She reached out and put her hand on top of his holding the spoon, preventing him from taking a bite.

He looked up at her, a single eyebrow lifted in challenge.

"Keep your voice down," she said. "Do you want to give them any more ideas? I'm sure Eiz'm is open to suggestions on more creative ways to break me."

They both knew the answer, but he shook his head all the same.

"I didn't think so." She released him and sat back. "Besides, I don't think that's why they did it."

"What other reason could they possibly have? Unless you're suggesting the king has a sadistic streak and just wanted to see us suffer, which I could totally buy."

"**No**. I don't know about you, but I was examined afterward. I think it was more research."

"Research for what?"

If only she knew. "How best to kill us?" she suggested.

"Doubtful. You honestly don't think they already know how to do that?"

She shot him a look. "What do you want me to say? I'm just as clueless as you. And speculating about their motives isn't getting us anywhere."

"You've spent more time with them."

"We've been over this. Just because I've shared a meal with him doesn't mean I get to hear his plans for humanity. I'm there for his amusement like a pet, not because he actually sees me as an equal."

"Well, you're not."

Was he *trying* to be an asshole today?

"*Thanks*," she snapped. "My point is, I don't know. And you need to stop insisting that I ever will. He's not stupid."

"But he is interested in you."

This again? Was he trying to be annoying? Or was he just as clueless about the situation as he was about her feelings for him?

"Think whatever you want, Ben. It doesn't matter, anyway."

"Maybe you just need to spend more time with him so gets comfortable and lets something slip."

"Look," she said forcefully, "I know you have tunnel vision for the escape mission, but you're sounding a lot like a pimp. So, cut it out, Ben."

His gaze softened a little, but the determination was still there. Nothing she said was going to make a difference. He was convinced she was the key to their chance at escape. Whether he meant to or not, Ben was siding with Knox. Which meant she officially had no one in her corner when it came to turning down dates with the alien king.

She was on her own, then.

14

KNOX

KNOX CLOSED his eyes and let the warmth seep through him. No one else was around. One of the perks of being king was he could reserve the solar incubator chamber. He had a smaller one in his suite but it wasn't as powerful as the public one. His father had chosen to prioritize the wellbeing of everyone rather than just himself as every good leader should do.

A beep sounded before the wall opened to reveal Dhaca. The guard seemed nervous, which was both odd and boded ill for whatever he had to say. "Excuse me, Your Majesty. If you're not busy at the moment, would you please come with me?"

Knox sat up. "What is it?"

"I know you said no harm was to come to the humans."

He didn't like where this was going. "*Yes?*"

"There's something you need to see."

Knox stood and followed him out.

Aerue was already waiting for him in the security room. He wore a frown and like he was debating on who would be reprimanded for something.

"If I may be excused, Your Majesty?" Dhaca cut in.

"Yes, of course," he answered, not taking his eyes off his friend. "What happened?"

"You'll want to sit down for this."

He did.

"Replay," Aerue commanded a technician, who had remained silent throughout the whole conversation.

Knox watched the split screen as both Verity and her Captain were brought into the same room at different times. When the water submerged both humans, he started to see red. What the hell was Dr. Mak'en thinking? Endangering the best candidates of the project, and in such a painful way? Especially since neither human was in the best health thanks to Eiz'm beating both of them. Breathing normally must be difficult, but to force them to hold their breath underwater for an indeterminate amount of time?

Unacceptable.

"Turn it off."

The technician did.

He turned back to Aerue. "Where is she?"

"Which one?"

"Dr. Mak'en." he answered. "Who did you think I was talking about?" He held up his hand. "Don't answer that."

He looked at the technician who was watching the conversation with ill-concealed interest. He should have had her leave before, and just have Awuth man the controls. He didn't need extra witnesses overhearing details of the project going awry.

"Leave us," he commanded.

The woman blushed, bowed, and left immediately.

"You know," Aerue started, "if you keep dismissing your people when we start discussing the project and a particular human female, they're going to start talking."

"You can tell me if they're gossiping about me. I'd rather know and call a meeting than have them spreading doubt and dissent while I'm unaware of the fact. Ignorance is not bliss. Let's not give it a chance to grow into something worse."

"Who would you like?"

"Everyone. From all departments." This wasn't a message just for his military. The most recent experiment proved his researchers also needed to hear it, and there was no harm in having more people receive his warning. No one was above him, and therefore no one could reject or disobey his commands.

"Including Eiz'm, Your Majesty?"

"No." The man would only sow dissent if he were present. He'd probably interrupt his speech and challenge his rule with an audience this time. Best to exclude him from the proceedings entirely. There was no reason to court chaos, and that's exactly what Eiz'm embodied. His absence would likely be noticed but it would be less disruptive.

"Understood. But what about the humans? Many of my men are guarding them. If I take them away to attend your meeting, the humans will be left unsupervised."

"Drop them all off in their rooms. They can't get out without someone letting them out, so they can be left unattended for a little while. Meals, interrogations, and tests are to be halted immediately. If Dr. Mak'en tries to argue, remind her it is an order from her king."

Aerue nodded. "Shall I assemble them in the hangar?"

Knox nodded. "I'll meet you there."

"Where are you going?"

He didn't respond, which was answer enough.

Aerue gave him a knowing look but wisely remained silent. He bowed and took his leave, off to gather his wayward subjects.

Knox pulled up the live feed of Verity's cell and watched her sleeping on her bed. She looked younger now than she did when she was awake. Likely due to the absence of her semipermanent scowl around him. She also lacked the hardness that came with the tension in her body, always ready to fight. In her sleep, she was only softness and he wanted to explore that more than was healthy.

But her breathing was labored and he felt anger rush through him yet again, remembering how his people had repeatedly harmed her. He hadn't been able to protect her.

He turned it off and removed it from the recently watched history. He didn't need anyone knowing what he did on his own.

He stood and made his way to the hangar. Almost no one was there yet, though he could hear them coming down the different corridors on their way. He forced himself to not pace the room. He wished the throne room was large enough to fit everyone. That way, he could be seated and the only nervous tick anyone would be able to see would be him tapping his fingers on the arm. And even that could be written off as impatience. There wasn't even a dais to raise him above everyone else.

"It has come to my attention," he started once his audience was in front of him. "That the safety and wellbeing of the subjects have been endangered not just during interrogations, but also during scientific tests. I thought I had made myself clear, but while answers of both natures are of the utmost importance, no one is allowed to potentially irreversibly harm them. If they are not alive and healthy, all of this will be for naught."

A guard raised his hand.

Knox sighed. "Yes?"

"Excuse me, Your Majesty, but can't we just grab more of them? There are billions on Earth as we speak."

"No, we cannot. Because the ones we have are already primed and truncate our study period. Even so, we are not yet ready to move on to the next stage and need them to accurately plan for when we eventually do broaden our scope to include the larger population of humanity. Now," he continued before another question could interrupt him, "from this point on, if *anyone* does something to jeopardize the subjects or the project, and therefore our future, they will be executed for treason."

He ignored Aerue's slight frown.

Silence greeted him.

"You're dismissed," he said.

The majority of his people left but the few other nobility on the ship remained. They rarely contributed anything useful other than bickering amongst themselves but based on their similar expressions it seemed they had come to some sort of consensus.

"With all due respect, Your Majesty," Quallokh said, "while we understand the wellbeing of the human subjects are important to you and your plan for us, isn't sacrificing our own a little extreme?"

Before he could answer, Zrelhlm added, "If you and your betrothed were to wed now and continue the line of succession, our dependence on your project would lessen. Would that not be a more satisfactory solution?"

"We've decided to postpone the wedding."

Again, he was met with stunned silence.

"She is not prepared to become a mother yet," if Arfilmea ever found out he'd shared that, she might kill him, "and I've been very focused on this project. As such, we will continue as we are and my earlier decree stands. The humans are to remain safe in our care. They are the key to our success. Does anyone have anything else to add?"

They all shook their heads though he could easily see his words had done nothing to diminish the doubt in their eyes.

"You may go, then," he said.

Once they were gone, Aerue approached him.

"Before you say anything, I know I need to be careful about appeasing people. But I expect people to obey my orders as their king, and this is nonnegotiable."

His friend nodded once. "I only hope they are worth it."

"They will be."

15

VERITY

AERUE RELEASED the restraints on her wrists. He took one in his hand and rolled each of her individual wrists, restoring circulation. "Thank you for your cooperation."

Verity didn't say anything. Her mouth was dry from talking so much and she had never felt worse about herself. She hadn't given away too much secret information this time. Today's session had started with questions about her father's work but then had become more focused on her, and she was forced to answer increasingly personal questions about her family. She had to wonder if Knox had specifically asked for them or if Aerue was just being thorough. Maybe if she knew the intimate details of the other STFs on base, she'd be forced to go just as in depth on their lives.

He walked her back to her room, and it took all her focus not to stumble with each step. They walked side by side and she saw him looking over at her a few times, likely shocked at her silence. She had no doubt that he'd be able to catch her if need be.

But she was too tired to make chit chat, or to needle him until he gave her a verbal reaction. She wanted nothing more than to go to sleep after that interrogation. He'd taken her right from lunch and he hadn't wasted any time in getting started. True to his word, he hadn't hurt her at all—not even to prompt an answer when she refused to open her mouth. That hadn't lasted too long, though, because he'd injected her with the same truth serum. Only, it was harder to resist this time. They had either supercharged it, or given her an extra large dose. She hadn't been able to get a good look at it before he'd plunged it into her arm.

Since neither of them could force a fast conclusion to their session, it dragged on forever, draining her more than she thought possible for such a humane interrogation. It was easy to understand why those tortured and starved would be exhausted, but she felt like a fraud since she'd barely suffered at all. Other than the mental pain of still selling out more details on her country's top-secret defense plans.

No one in the government even knew that she was so aware of her father's work. She'd never left his side as a child but even when he used to bring her to his meetings in SCIFs against other officers' objections when she was a girl, he had always given her something else to entertain herself with. But he had been given special permission from the higher ups—not that there were many above him given the level of secrecy surrounding the whole protocol—to bring work home from time to time. He'd be across from her at the dining room table while she did her homework. It was enough for her to pick up on a lot of things even though he kept the vow of silence he made seriously. So, while he never *told* her anything, she still knew more than anyone else not directly involved in the planning of an anti-alien response. ASE was in charge of the science end of things and were responsible for handling a peaceful encounter, but now that was clearly shot to hell after these aliens snatched no only civilians and personnel from ASE and the STF.

Though why Knox thought it wasn't that big of an issue still confused her. Eiz'm clearly wanted a fight, and she couldn't tell where Aerue stood on the issue. He seemed like he'd likely back

Knox no matter what but was equally ready to take up arms—not that she'd seen any of their weaponry yet—the moment it was required.

The door to her room opened and instead of a new set of plain clothes, a forest green dress with a lace bodice and tulle skirt. There were also a matching pair of flats. Too bad. A heel could've been a weapon. Which was probably why they hadn't given them to her.

There was no note but also no doubt about where it had come from. She glanced back at Aerue who was in the process of releasing her wrists.

He looked up and shrugged. She wasn't sure she believed his ignorance act, but he clearly wasn't going to comment on his king's decision to make her play dress up. He did say, "I'll pick you up for dinner. You have time to rest."

It stung that he knew she was exhausted. She needed to hide her emotions better. Sure, she'd been taught how to fight with and without weapons at her father's insistence, and learned basic spy skills, but her dad had barred her from been admitted to the interrogation classes where the STFs were taught what to do both as interrogator and victim. Even if she had been, she doubted he would've let them go all the way in the training. And nothing could prepare them for the alien truth serum of which there seemed to be an endless supply. Aerue had given her a larger dose today than Eiz'm had the day before, probably to make up for the inability to force answers out of her through other methods.

The absurd image of Knox picking out and buying a dress from Earth entered her mind, but given how they had created human food, it was much more likely that they had created it from scratch after researching human style, or someone on this ship personally had a decidedly human taste in fashion.

She picked it up and moved it to the foot of the bed so she could sleep.

Verity wasn't sure how much later it was when she opened her eyes, but the knock on the door was all the warning she got from Aerue before it opened. "You're not dressed yet."

"I was sleeping." He'd already assumed she would earlier, so there was no harm in confirming it. When he didn't look away, she added, "Give me a moment to change."

Finally, he turned around.

Verity waited until the door closed between them then hastily put on the dress. What she had assumed was a delicate lace bodice was actually a tight fabric that perfectly molded to her body despite not being stretchy. She glanced up at the ceiling, searching again for cameras. How else would they know her measurements so perfectly? It was like a secret bodycon dress, restricting her movement much more than she would've liked. She had no doubt it was a calculated move.

But as much as it reigned her in, it also provided an unexpected amount of support, especially around the bodice. It was like wearing a nicer version of a corset. She'd worn a real one for one Halloween and vowed never again. Right now, this was providing enough compression to not feel like her ribs were aching, but also just a little too tight and making it hard to breathe. Scratch that. It was just like a normal corset.

"Ready?" Aerue said impatiently. Well, she assumed it was, even though his tone never changed. One of these days, she wanted proof that he could emote, though she wasn't willing to make him angry like she was with Eiz'm. If Aerue's ability to be patient and draw things out also applied to his fighting style, she didn't want to be his opponent. At least with the hot-headed Eiz'm, she could expect a quick knockout punch.

"Yes," she answered.

He turned around, not even looking at her outfit, and cuffed her up again before marching her down the corridor. But they weren't going in the same direction as the mess hall, the throne room, or even the dining room where she'd been before.

"You know," she said, "If he wanted a show, he should've given me something that showed more skin." It's not like she'd have an option to wear it unless she wanted to stay in the barely tolerable prison clothes. Even though they gave her a new pair every morning, they were made of stiff fabric and were always made her slightly itchy.

She didn't turn when the door closed behind her, instead taking her new surroundings. This room was much smaller, though still grand, especially in comparison to her room. A table and chairs were set up with a large cut of meat and two settings complete with knives and forks for both of them—a first since she'd been stuck on this godforsaken ship—but the king was nowhere to be found.

Aerue released her from her bindings but stayed close behind her, no doubt ready to restrain her again at a moment's notice. If he wasn't an enemy, she'd admire his vigilance. And if he were human, he would make a good asset to the Air Force or Army, though her dad would likely write him off as a jarhead.

Then she heard the heavy breathing. She turned and saw a gap in the wall. A secret entrance she would have otherwise missed amidst the opulence of the room.

Aerue cursed behind her but didn't stop her from taking a step closer. Inside, she saw Knox naked on his bed, fucking a woman. Every time he moved, she caught a glimpse of a purple-blue chrome sheen on his skin—like the Milky Way, if her galaxy really were a liquid like its name suggested. But it didn't look like sweat coating him. If anything, it looked embedded in or beneath the surface.

Shock held her immobile. Witnessing what they were doing—and for it to be so similar to humans—momentarily made her mind go blank. Verity felt her body heat with equal parts arousal and disgust. She should have looked away, but she couldn't bring herself to.

Likely feeling her stare, the woman met her gaze and smiled.

Arfilmea.

Barely a second passed before Knox glanced over. If he was surprised at her appearance, he didn't show it. His pace didn't falter at all, and he quickly turned his attention back to his lover.

Verity turned and leaned against the wall, closing her eyes. She couldn't stand to watch any more or to see Aerue's reaction to her spying on his sister and his king.

If the king didn't want an audience, he shouldn't have invited her. And why the hell was he having dinner with her when he already had his betrothed to entertain him.

Her traitorous mind wondered if his bed was as soft as it looked, like a cloud she could sink into and never want to leave. The image of him sleeping there invaded her mind and even worse, it combined with her first thought and suddenly she was picturing him pressing *her* into the mattress with his body lying on top of her. She should've been repulsed but to her horror, she felt her breasts grow heavy and her nipples tighten.

She mentally shook herself. It didn't matter. The only reason she was interested was because she'd been sleeping on a raised hard futon for a few days and she missed her own bed.

Even though she couldn't see it anymore, she could still hear them. She wanted to gag. In fact, she wasn't sure she wouldn't before the night was over. If she thought Aerue would take her to the mess hall, she would've asked for the plain and suspect prisoner food rather than deal with Knox right then.

"I'll see you later?"

Arfilmea murmured the words so softly she was surprised she could hear them at all.

Knox, ass that he clearly was, didn't answer.

A door closed, and curiosity got the better of her. She looked in and saw him getting dressed alone in the room. His fingers moved quickly over his shirt's buttons. Then the jerk turned around as he was pulling on a pair of pants with nothing underneath, giving her a good look at the impressive and semi-hard cock between his legs.

Her body reacted swiftly, only making the situation more mortifying and infuriating. She turned and stalked towards the window. Aerue shadowed her but there was no reason to. It's not like she could go anywhere else. She was already the farthest she could get from the king without leaving the private dining room. She forced herself to take deep breaths. God, she wanted to castrate him. Maybe that would make him take her seriously.

Verity stared out into space and wished she was sitting at the old wooden table in her dining room waiting for her dad to come home for dinner. Anything but being here would be better.

She felt Knox's gaze on her body as he walked out of the room and towards her. She finally turned her attention back to him, catching the moment his galaxy eyes lifted from her chest back to her face. Maybe Ben was right about the king's interest in her after all.

She examined him, too. It was only fair. In the time she hadn't been watching, he'd pulled on a green suit and tie that matched her dress and it hugged his body so well that there was no doubt as to how fit he was, even if she hadn't just accidentally seen him naked. It was absurd how well he looked in human clothing. What were his alien clothes like? She bet he looked as striking in those as he did right now.

The corner of his mouth lifted in a smirk. If he thought she was going to make a comment about his appearance or catching him *in flagrante delicto*, he would be disappointed. It was the shock more than anything that had got her. It's not like she wasn't used to hearing the base's STFs brag about their sexual conquests. Once they'd gotten over her being a girl and the General's daughter, they had completely obliterated their filters in front of her.

She held her head high and silently sat down before he could come near her, wincing as the sudden movement hurt her ribs.

He frowned, no doubt unhappy that he'd been cheated of the opportunity to show his manners in pulling out her chair and other signs of largely-dead chivalry. He took his own seat and stared at her unashamed.

It took everything to not give into her urge to look away or hide. It wasn't that she was embarrassed by her body but she wasn't used to people looking at her with such explicit interest. On the base, she was off limits, and at school, she often wore baggy clothes on top of her form-fitting dance clothes to keep her muscles warm after classes. It really cut down on the number of people who could or *would* openly admire her.

Aerue walked past her and whispered something to Knox so quietly that she could barely eavesdrop, but given "show" she heard and the king's smile returning, she bet it was her comment about the dress.

He said something in reply and Aerue backed away, gave her a piercing look, then left the room. It was the first time she'd been left alone with him, and Aerue clearly wasn't a huge fan of the decision.

But with his personal guard finally gone, so maybe she could finally take this alien king on. The dress was pretty, but it wasn't worth more than her freedom. If she had to rip it, so be it.

Reading her intentions, he quietly murmured, "I wouldn't try anything if I were you. I'd hate to ruin dinner before it's even begun."

She bit back the retort on the tip of her tongue: *You already did that all by yourself.*

16

KNOX

KNOX HEARD AERUE LEAVE. He hadn't been able to take his eyes off Verity since he'd entered the room. He had expected her to fight the dinner invitation and especially the dress. He wouldn't have been surprised if she'd shown up in her regular clothes just to spite him, but he was very glad she hadn't taken that route. To say he was pleasantly surprised with her appearance was an understatement. Even though he could still see faint bruising on her cheeks and her hair was beautiful despite being unpolished, she looked as elegant as Arfilmea had at galas they used to have on their planet. There hadn't been a party since they boarded the ship, but—humanity aside—Verity would fit right in. He hadn't been entirely sure how she would look in it, though he had complete faith in his dresser to make an outstanding outfit.

As good as she looked in the fabric, he now wanted it off and on the ground. He hadn't meant for her to walk in on him and Arfilmea, and he would've tried to avoid it had he thought it was a possibility, but he was almost happy she had. It was the most unguarded reaction he'd seen from her in the whole time he'd known her. And though she was definitely pissed at him—for what specifically, he wasn't sure—her desire was unmistakable in her pert nipples and dilated eyes.

It was a shame that she hadn't commented on it. He would've loved to hear what verbal barbs she would've thrown to deflect from her natural reaction.

He was tempted to provoke her, but he didn't want to spoil their meal. It was their first in a while and he had genuinely merely wanted the pleasure of her company. He needed to get them back on safe territory.

Once she was ready, however, he couldn't wait to take her to bed. She promised to be fiery and explosive lover. He couldn't wait to be engulfed in her heat.

For all her sniping at him, Arfilmea was surprisingly passive when it came to fucking. She preferred for him to do most of the work, not that he minded. But based on the glare Verity was giving him, she would be the same in and out of bed: giving back anything he gave her. It would probably be more *war* than love with her, and that was fine with him. Exciting, even.

He bit back a smile. No need to show the human in question how amused he was. She'd only use it to pick another fight, and even though certain things remained off limits, there were much more pleasant things to do now that they were alone. He stood and poured them each a drink and handed hers back.

She took the cup carefully and was diligent in not letting their fingers touch. He hadn't expected her to be so shy about physical touch but maybe her bravado was just that. What else would explain her avoidance like avoidance like a nervous virgin? Unless she was one?

The idea went straight to his cock, hardening it to an almost painful degree. He took a sip, sighing as the sweet flavor danced over his tongue. It was supposedly an aphrodisiac though he'd never experienced it that way. He hoped it didn't prove him wrong tonight. He was already incredibly aroused and if he became any more so, he might do something rash. Like offer to make a meal out of her and forget the actual food.

She stared at her goblet but didn't pick it up, no doubt suspicious of it the same way she had been of every meal she'd eaten so far.

"It's perfectly safe to drink. And there are no sedatives in it like your human alcohol."

When she didn't move to try it, he took another sip of his and saw the moment an idea popped into her head.

Without saying a word, she leaned forward, showing him more of her body than she would ever willingly do, and swapped their goblets. She looked him in the eye before drinking from what had been his cup only seconds ago. As he watched her delicate throat swallow the liquid, he couldn't help but notice that mouth closed over the exact same spot where his had. He wondered if she even realized it. He held in the groan that threatened to escape when she licked some stray drops from her lips.

He should've asked one of his scientists what the drink would do to her. An egregious oversight on his part, although he was sure no harm could come of it. But would *she* feel the lascivious side effects? If she did, would it be the same as what his kind felt or would it be at a different level? She was already aroused, so who knew if the drink would stoke that desire even higher?

He looked away before she set the cup down and could notice his staring. "What do you think?"

"It's sweet." She swirled the glass around and watched, seemingly mesmerized. "And a lot thicker than most drinks on Earth. It reminds me of honey."

"Is that bad?"

"No, but it's not something we drink on its own. Well," she smiled. "Most people don't. But I've always had a sweet tooth." The smile dropped, as if she realized she'd shared more than she meant to.

Aerue had said he'd used a larger dose of their truth serum on her today, but its effects should've worn off by now. Perhaps it was a genuine slip, or she was attempting to manipulate him. If that were the case, she was more successful than he would've liked. He was inexplicably desperate for her to personally open up and it was starting to concern him almost as much as it did his friend. But he'd watched the recording of their session today and she had opened up a lot about her family. It seemed she really had no idea about the secrets that lay in her genetics. He wondered how she would react once she finally learned the truth. Badly, most likely. Though her anger might not be directed at him in that instance.

Inviting Arfilmea over had been a distraction so he could finally get Verity out of his mind and meet her for dinner with a cool head, but he'd found himself imagining it was her instead of his betrothed beneath him more than a few times. And once he'd caught her watching in the doorway? His mind had been firmly possessed by her once more.

"What is it?" she asked, pulling him back to the present. She took another small sip and licked her lips. "It reminds me of ambrosia. Well, I think it does."

"What's that?" He knew the answer already, but he wanted to hear her explanation. She didn't seem the kind of person to believe in anything other than facts, so her talking about mythology should be interesting. He picked up his new glass and lifted an eyebrow as he took another drink.

She narrowed her eyes but humored him and answered anyway. "Food of the Greek gods. It doesn't matter. And answer the question, *Your Majesty*."

He rose again and stood closer to Verity, enjoying the way she leaned away from the table and sat straighter as if worried he'd reach out and touch her.

Was she worried of his potential action or her reaction to it?

From underneath the table, he pulled out a carving knife and large fork. Aerue hadn't been keen on the idea of having any sharp objects near Verity—not her eating utensils, much less the serving set he now held in his hands—but he had still left when Knox had sent him away.

He started cutting the meat into thin slices. "It's a delicacy normally reserved for nobility."

Without looking, he knew that his human guest was staring at the would-be weapon in his hand. No doubt she was calculating her chances of using it against him. Which was why he planned on stowing it back in the table's secret compartment on his side. That way, she wouldn't be able to find it and wield it against him should he experience a moment of weakness with her and let his guard down.

"So, I guess I was right." She smiled wryly at him. "I must be very special, then, if you're giving me—a human—an honor even your subjects don't get to enjoy."

She had no idea. He didn't miss the forced nature of her light tone. She might be more accommodating tonight than ever before, but she still looked at him like she never wanted to be closer than striking distance of him. If she was afraid that *he* would hurt her, she needn't be, but he wondered if there was another reason she stayed clear of him.

He was always simultaneously drawn in by her uniqueness and repelled by the potential danger she posed. Though he wasn't afraid she could actually hurt him, he still didn't want to give her an opportunity after her failed attempt during their first meeting.

And with Aerue gone right now, if she went on the offensive, he'd have to personally fight her.

The dress would likely hinder her, but he had no doubt she'd rip it or strip out of it to accomplish her goal. After all, he'd already seen her do it in the water tank.

"What is that?" she finally asked, gesturing to his work.

"I suppose it's similar to your cows and horses." They were also incredibly rare and there had been a lot of discussion with the chef about eating one tonight with a *human* who wouldn't appreciate its specialness. But he hadn't argued with him, once he'd insisted. At least some people on his ship still respected his rule.

Maybe his ancestors had been right in being harsher in their reigns. He still wasn't willing to go as far as his grandfather, but perhaps taking a page out of his father's handbook would be a good idea. Dissent was dangerous, and if Aerue was right, it was already spreading like a cancer. Something beyond his verbal admonition had to be done. Even as he'd given his speech in the hangar, he could sense his words went unheeded by some in the room.

She leaned forward, the movement slower and stiffer than the grace he'd seen in her during their breakfast, and placed an elbow on the table and resting her cheek in her hand. "You know those aren't that similar, right?"

His eyes narrowed. She was clearly in more pain than she was letting on. Eiz'm hadn't been near her since he'd beaten her, but two weeks was not enough time to heal the harm he'd done to her ribs. His eyes drifted to her torso, the part that wasn't blocked by the table, and wished he could see how bad the damage was. He flicked his gaze back up to her, but she didn't give any signal to indicate she'd noticed his examination. He had already planned to give her something for the pain, but now he was glad he'd prepared more than needed for a single bruise, even one that had formed as a result of repeated hits by one of his kind.

To her comment, he shrugged. "It's also an endangered species." He ignored the questioning look she gave him as he cut the final piece and sat down, storing the razor sharp knife and fork where she couldn't see. He gestured to the plate. "Ladies first, as I believe the saying goes."

She smiled. "Let's go with royalty first."

"Still don't trust that I'm not trying to poison you?"

"One can never be too careful."

He smiled, and took a piece for himself. "Very true." He took a bite and sighed. The last time he'd eaten this was at his coronation. And that had been ages ago.

He watched for her reaction as she took her first bite and felt a burst of pride as her eyes closed in ecstasy. He'd never seen someone so passionate about food before. When they opened again, they weren't quite as sharp as before.

"What do you think?"

"That this is a lot more delicious than what you made me believe. You've clearly never eaten Earthly meat before." She cut another piece from her plate and ate it quickly.

"My mistake." He smiled. "I'm glad you enjoy it so much."

She took another sip of her drink and he did the same. It felt oddly normal for them to eat together, even though it was only their second time, and the first time without being interrupted. He hoped she was enjoying herself as much as he was and this could become a new routine for them both.

"You still haven't told me where you're from or why you've come to Earth."

"Much farther than your space programs can hope to reach within the next century."

She raised an eyebrow, no doubt taking it as a challenge.

"Our planet became uninhabitable and your planet bore the most similarity," he added. There was no harm in knowing a little bit more about his history. Of course, not just the *planet* but also the people, but he wasn't about to share that information.

"And you're going to wipe out humanity so you can have the planet to yourselves?"

"I have never confirmed this malevolent assumption of yours, and I don't know why you keep insisting I'm presiding over a genocidal mission."

"Sorry. I'm still getting over being kidnapped in the middle of the night. It only confirmed ideas that are prevalent on Earth."

"But you are starting to get over it?"

"Don't get ahead of yourself." Despite the content of her words, they lacked her usual antagonistic fire. Another good sign that she was starting to like him more.

"What theories does it support, then?"

"Most of them are alien overlords enslave humanity in one way or another. And if you're unaware, I'm from a country that's very against slavery." She made a face. "Well, most of us are. But not everyone and not always."

"Oh?"

"Human history is complicated."

He was well aware, though he didn't say anything else on the matter. "Can you tell me more about yourself?"

Her easy demeanor disappeared, and she rolled her shoulders back as if entering into battle.

"I would've assumed Eiz'm and Aerue would have told you."

"I truly apologize for Eiz'm. As you may recall, I told him not to hurt you."

She didn't answer, but she couldn't deny that's what had happened.

"I hope things were better with Aerue today. And that's not what I asked."

"You know my name, my age, and my family. You also now know way too much about my father's work. What else is there for you to know?"

"What makes you happy?"

"Being with friends and family, dancing," she hesitated before adding, "and writing." Her eyes darted to the left as she said the last part, a sign she was likely lying.

He didn't call her on it. He'd play along. "Would you like the opportunity to write in your free time?"

Her mouth dropped open. "You'd do that for me?"

It might be a mistake, but he nodded. He'd have one of the lower guards do it. He didn't need a lecture from Aerue.

"That would be amazing. Thank you."

He held his glass out to her, and she brought her own up to clink them together. They both drank at the same time and he was glad they'd finally reached an agreement on something.

17

VERITY

VERITY DIDN'T TALK MUCH MORE after Knox had agreed to give her writing supplies. She didn't know how long the truth serum lasted and had already shared too much about liking sugar and writing, even though it was also advantageous to her plan to secretly communicate with Ben when they weren't together.

But her silence hadn't killed the mood like she expected it to. Though the fact that there *was* a mood to begin with was still disconcerting. This felt like an actual date rather than a meal between captor and captive. It was messed up on so many levels that she was starting to actually trust him despite everything he'd done to her and those she cared about.

Once she cleaned her plate and eaten her fill she pushed her plate away. He did the same, even though there was still some food on his. Then, to her surprise, he cleared their plates and placed them on the lower level of a separate table she hadn't noticed.

What he placed before her was a colorless gelatin-like substance and she wondered if it was like a Japanese raindrop cake, not that she'd ever eaten one. Nor would she ever choose to since she couldn't stand eating slimy pudding or similar textures.

"I promise it's more flavorful than it looks."

She looked up and saw him watching her with an amused smile. For the first time ever, she wasn't immediately tempted to wipe it off his face. "Can you tell me more about what to expect? Do you have another Earthly comparison to make?"

"That didn't go so well last time, so I think I'll let you tell me after you've tried it." Still standing next to her, he took her glass and refilled it.

She would have assumed he was trying to get her drunk if not for his assurance that it had no sedative properties and proven his word with her own experience. At the very least, if he'd lied it was the slowest acting depressant she'd ever experienced, so unlike their truth telling serum which took effect even as it was still leaving the syringe.

He went back to his seat and filled his own glass.

Verity looked back down at her plate and tentatively cut into it, half expecting it to gush all over her plate. She held his gaze as she brought the piece to her mouth. Like the drink, it was incredibly sweet and not the texture she'd been expecting. If anything, it felt like eating cotton candy without the sticky residue which always left her licking her fingers and mouth to get every last trace of sugar. She was glad not to have to do that here. She'd seen him watching her drink before and his reaction to her automatically licking her lips. And as great as it was to have further confirmation that she was affecting him, his reaction had affected *her* more than was helpful.

Even though she'd only shared her preference for sweet things to him less than thirty minutes ago, she wondered if he had somehow already had that information. How else would he know to make the entire menu so perfectly tailored to her taste? Even the meat had been sweet in its own way. She highly doubted the average alien had that much more of a sweet tooth than the average human. Especially if he was telling the truth about their homes being similar, which only added more credibility to the still outlandish possibility that their species were a near-perfect example of convergent evolution.

His plate was untouched. He was clearly waiting for her reaction.

She tried to think of a neutral word that would keep them in safe territory. "Delicious," she said.

His galaxy eyes heated, transforming from light violet to a darker purple. Clearly, she'd chosen wrong but it was too late to take back now.

"I'm glad," he said. She watched him take a bite, unwilling to break their eye contact first, even though it felt like exposing her very soul to him.

He finally looked away but smiled as if he'd still won the small victory. She glared at him as he reached for his cup. Maybe he'd choke on it.

He placed it back down and raised an eyebrow at her. "Is something wrong?"

Yes. This entire situation. She forced a smile and shook her head. There was no reason for him to know how much she still resented him, and worse, her growing attraction to him. The first would ruin any progress she'd made in him softening towards her and the second would go right to his head. And he was already too cocky for her own good.

Verity continued eating, and hoped he wasn't hiding yet another course. At this rate, she'd gain weight in no time. "I thought of another option." The words were already out before she could think better than letting him know that she'd figured out his master plan.

"About why we're here?" he asked, not missing a beat.

"You're going to eat us."

He sighed. "What gave you that idea?"

"You're trying to fatten me up. Like Hansel and Gretel."

Her skin heated under his leisurely perusal just like it had at the start of the meal.

"Not at all," he finally answered. "And I do not know who these people you mentioned are."

How could he know English, some human food but not others, and clothes suspiciously well, but not one of the most popular fairytales ever? "Never mind."

"Is it important?"

"No." A fairytale wasn't exactly a state secret and therefore probably was of no interest to him. Even if it was, she wouldn't tell him now that she clearly had control over her words again. Relatively speaking. He still seemed to have some power over her that constantly removed her filter. Which needed to be sorted out soon before she did more damage than she could undo.

She cleaned her plate quickly, hoping the meal would end as soon as she did and she could get away from him until the next time he summoned her.

She was right.

Knox stood and she did the same. "Thank you for spending tonight with me."

A meal was not the same as the whole night. *That* would involve going to another room, which only made her blush. Did he understand the connotations of those words? His sincere expression made her think not.

"Of course," she said. "Thank you for inviting me."

And then his hand touched the small of her back and led her towards the door, proving her wrong. He wasn't done with her yet after all.

At least it wasn't the door to his bedroom.

They walked past Aerue who was standing outside. She glanced back at him and took in his sour expression before looking forward again. "He doesn't like me very much."

"He'll get over it."

Not the most comforting words, though why it mattered to her at all was pointless. As long as he didn't injure her, how his right hand felt about her was irrelevant.

She counted the number of doors they passed on the way back to her room, rather than focusing on how his body heat was warming her from head to toe as they walked side by side.

When they reached her room, he didn't open the door, denying her the quick escape she'd been hoping for once it became clear he was personally escorting her back.

She refused to turn toward him. If she could look at his face this close up, she was worried that instead of punching him, she'd do something even stupider. Like kiss him.

He held her arms and took the choice out of her hands when he rotated her so he could look her in the eye.

She saw him pull a vial out of his jacket pocket. He handed it to her and she lifted it up to the light. It was orange unlike the clear truth serum. Unless he'd decided to disguise it in hopes that she'd spill her guts in her sleep. Though she'd never been a sleep talker, who knew the full effects of these alien drugs?

"It's a healing elixir." She pulled back when his hand cupped her cheek. "You put it on your injuries." His thumb brushed over her bruise and she couldn't help but flinch.

His eyebrows knit together and the corners of his mouth turned down. He seemed genuinely upset that she was in pain, though she still couldn't think of a reasonable motive for him to feel that way.

He tilted his head down, placing his lips dangerously close to hers. It would be so easy for him to kiss her now—or for her to kiss him. "I am sorry he hurt you," he murmured.

"Thank you," she replied, equally as quiet, not wanting to break the spell.

"You rub it into the affected area and it should be healed by morning. A few drops should do the trick."

She searched his gaze for any signs of deception but came up empty.

He opened his mouth, then closed it, as if deciding against what he was going to say. "Goodnight, Verity."

She didn't even have the energy to correct him and say only friends were allowed to call her that.

"Goodnight." She breathed the word more than said it, and she was surprised her voice carried the sound at all, her throat was so dry.

He opened the door for her and she walked in without looking back at him. Only when she heard it shut behind her did she turn around.

She looked down at the vial in her hand. Even if he was telling the truth, she wasn't putting it on her face. At least, not yet. She got undressed and placed the folded dress on the shelf. Then she shook two droplets out onto her fingers. It felt like massage oil. Holding her breath, she rubbed it into the skin covering her aching ribs then changed into her regular plain clothes. If it worked, great. If not, she hoped it wasn't secretly doing something worse.

She climbed into bed and stared up at the ceiling. She'd finally gotten more information from Knox about his history, but it was barely enough of a lead to be worth mentioning to ASE, much less anyone on the base once she got home. Still, it was better than the nothing she had started with before dinner.

She closed her eyes and willed sleep to take her. She got her wish within minutes.

VERITY WAS ALREADY awake by the time the guards came knocking. She had checked her ribs first thing and was shocked to see that they were healed just like Knox had promised. She'd quickly applied some to her face, and palmed the vial and slid it up her sleeve as they bound her wrists together. She didn't want any of the guards taking it away from her if they found it in her room.

It was a little sad how quickly she'd gotten used to the routine, but there wasn't much else she could do until she had a more complete plan in place to escape. Who was she kidding? She need **a** plan, period.

Yet again, she arrived before Ben and was halfway through her meal when he finally arrived. Once she was sitting and her escort had walked away, she slid the vial into her waistband so she could eat normally without raising suspicions. She'd already eaten like—well, royalty—last night, but she'd woken up starving. Maybe it was the elixir. Who knew? But she felt fine, so she wasn't going to look any further into it.

He was walking funny. He always moved easily that reminded her of a dancer even though he didn't believe in how rigorous dancers' fitness routines were. They disagreed on it a lot, but she knew they only brought it up now to needle the other. After all, she was a dancer, and it had definitely helped her dodge more attacks than some of the STFs.

But the way he was walking reminded her of new recruits after they had their asses beat during fight training. And Ben was way beyond that point. Which meant that he'd come up against Eiz'm again, and the ass hadn't held back.

He sat down as stiffly as she'd felt the night before, which only confirmed what she'd already guessed. But she wanted to hear his side of the story. "What happened?"

"What do you think?"

She nodded. "Did they give you anything?"

"It happened the same as you said."

"Did you give them anything?"

"No. I held my breath until I passed out. The bastard wasn't cooperating in knocking me out like he did for you. He got smarter after you pulled that stunt."

"Sorry." But at least Ben had been able to also outsmart Eiz'm. "When?"

"Last night during dinner. At least they gave me food afterward. Couldn't keep much of it down, though."

Her blood ran cold. How had she not seen it before? The fancy dinner had been nothing more than an elaborate ruse to keep her from asking questions. If she'd been at dinner with all the other humans, there would've been no way for her not to notice Ben's absence. And to think that she'd been warming up to Knox while he had his vicious interrogator attacking her best friend. Though that was probably the exact reason for splitting them up.

The king had to know that they were friends. Most of the guards here barely paid any attention to the other prisoners but she'd lost count how many times at least one glanced their way. They'd been stupid by being too obvious, and Ben had paid for their mistake.

"I had no idea," she said.

"Weren't you here?"

She shook her head. "The king invited me for dinner. Now we know why."

Ben grunted. "Was it worth it?"

"He said his home world became uninhabitable and that ours is very similar so that's why they've come."

"Do you believe him?"

"Yes." Though she wasn't sure if she should now that some of his ulterior motives had been revealed. "But that's all the information I could pry out of him."

"Did he get anything else out of you?"

"No." Nothing important, anyway. Something told her Ben would lecture her about sharing *anything* personal and she didn't feel like hearing it.

She pulled the hidden vial out with one hand and tapped the table twice with the other.

His warm hand met hers underneath the table, sending warmth through her arm with the intensity and speed of a lightening strike. She let go and withdrew her hand.

Verity didn't have to tell him not to look at it now, but she saw the question in his eyes as he no doubt was trying to guess what it was based on touch.

"It's a healing elixir," she whispered as softly as possible, repeating the king's explanation. "You rub it into the affected area and it should be healed by morning."

He frowned. "Do you trust it?"

"I tested it last night and it obviously worked. Without side effects, too."

He wasn't appeased. "I don't want anything from them."

"Get over yourself, Ben. We both need to be healthy."

"Do we have a plan?"

She shook her head. "But the king promised to give me writing tools." Then again, he'd been duplicitous in the timing of Ben's interrogation and her dinner with him, so she couldn't exactly count on that now. "But if not, I'll think of another way to communicate with you even when we're not at a meal. Too bad we're never left alone or I could knock on your door as the signal."

"Why not?"

"I'm sure you could take them out quickly enough for it to not matter. And we're all in our rooms when we're not eating or being interrogated."

"Have you talked to the others?"

He shook his head. "We're all constantly monitored. I can't even move from this table without the guards getting involved. From what I gathered, they take us in groups to be interrogated, and not everyone gets the asshole questioning them. I guess they save him for us. And from the looks of it, none of them seem to be beaten up as badly as us. I think they're talking more during their sessions."

"But most of them are civvies. They don't know what they're saying."

"Which is probably to our advantage against them. But they also are clearly smart enough to sic the meanest interrogator on us, so they also can recognize that *we* have actual information. And I don't know how many more times I can cut off my own oxygen."

She nodded. They needed to get home sooner rather than later, or even she and Ben would start talking and doom their planet.

18

KNOX

KNOX STRODE through the corridor until he reached the door he was looking for. He knocked twice and opened the door after silence met him. He stepped inside and found the man he was looking for deep in thought.

The human Captain—Benjamin Tenner—sat on his bed, elbows resting on his knees, his chin resting on clasped hands. He didn't even turn to look at him, as he'd somehow expected him, though that was impossible. "You must be the king," he said, his tone flat and seemingly disinterested.

"I am," Knox said. How interesting. If the human already knew who he was, then he likely also blamed him for Verity's maltreatment. He half-expected the man to rush at him, and he'd been looking forward in seeing the man's abilities. "I have a few questions for you."

He smirked. "Didn't get enough from me yesterday?"

Knox smiled. He could easily picture Verity saying the same thing. But he'd be much happier hearing it from her than this human.

He and Benjamin were both perfectly aware that he hadn't given up anything, taking a page out of Verity's book by incapacitating himself while taking a beating from Eiz'm. He'd done it during his first interrogation after she had told him in the cafeteria, and again every time since.

He should be mad at his colonel for losing control yet again with one of the project's best candidates, especially since such severe and repeated damage would become irreversible at some point, but he couldn't muster the same outrage. If Aerue could hear his thoughts, his friend would question him again about his differential treatment of Verity in comparison to the other humans.

But couldn't allow the man to permanently injure himself in the process of thwarting their interrogation tactics. Asking Eiz'm to take it easy on yet another human would raise red flags and asking Aerue to do it would take up too much of his personal guard's time. And despite his friend's new penchant for lecturing him, he still needed his right hand available. The only reason he was ever otherwise occupied was because he didn't trust anyone enough to handle Verity without resorting to violence.

Knox walked farther into the room, standing in front of the man, but far enough out of reach that there would be plenty of time to evade or mount a counterattack should Benjamin choose to have a go at him. "You're a Captain in your country's Air Force." The uniform he'd been captured in had been a dead giveaway, but he wanted confirmation.

The man gave him nothing but he wasn't pulling the same trick he had in interrogation. Perhaps being in a more neutral and less antagonistic space was helping yield better results. There was still hope he, unlike Eiz'm, could get an actual answer, even without using the truth serum. Tenner and Verity's ability to withstand its effects long enough to enact their creative work arounds was proof enough that the serum was less effective on them than on the less viable subjects, and even on his own kind. Perhaps it was their hybrid nature that gave them partial immunity.

"Your father was an airman before he died, and you grew up with the other children on base." He was only interested in one, but he didn't say it. Nor did it seem he needed to based on the human's frown.

They were both acutely aware of the third person between them, even if she wasn't physically in the room with them at the moment.

Trohm's inside information on the Captain also told him that the human viewed Major General Landau as a second father. Did that mean he viewed Verity as a sister and nothing more? "Did you always want to be an airman?"

There was no hesitation. "Yes."

"And what are your responsibilities?"

The human remained silent.

Perhaps Knox had been premature in his optimism. If anything, the Captain seemed even more belligerent now than he did during his interrogations. There, he was merely stubborn. Right now, he looked like he wanted to go on the attack.

Trohm had regularly informed him that military people were intelligent in addition to strong, but from what he'd seen so far, it seemed like the human was more brawn than brains compared to Verity's mind over matter. Not to say that either of them was genuinely *lacking* one aspect completely. It was all relative.

But the Captain was holding himself back for some reason. Because he likely knew he couldn't win. Perhaps the man was smarter than he appeared.

Rather than push for an answer, Knox moved on to his next question. "How often does information leak to individuals not directly involved in a specific mission?" Verity wasn't part of the Air Force, but she seemed to know more details than he would expect based on her unofficial affiliation. And it was different information than the space scientists had given so far. Clearly, Earth's response to extraterrestrial forces was very compartmentalized.

Was Verity's depth of knowledge a secret between her and her father, or did other people know? At the very least, he expected this man to know. They were best friends, after all.

The human shook his head. "There are no leaks."

"And yet you've asked what Miss Landau has divulged. She's not involved in any of the planning or implementation of the plans. If there are no breaches of secrecy as you claim, wouldn't she be completely ignorant and therefore have nothing to hide?"

A muscle ticked in the human's jaw, the first visible sign that he was being affected by his questions. He then stood suddenly without any sign of discomfort. The man seemed to be handling it much better than he expected, as if he weren't in any pain at all. Or, he was much better at schooling his expression.

The mostly likely explanation was Verity must have given him some of the healing elixir. Was she always so generous or was it this particular human that made her altruistic?

"If you're trying to use her to get information from me," the human said, "it won't work. And if you use her in *any* way, there will be hell to pay from her, from me, and her father."

Knox nodded, though the threat was a rather empty one given his guards had the situation under control and the general was very far away on Earth and likely in no fighting shape after his encounter with Eiz'm.

"Understood." He could practically see the defensive walls coming up between them. He'd try again at another time. "Thank you for your cooperation, Lieutenant."

The human didn't answer, nor did he sit back down. He merely stared at him, his hatred apparent in his eyes.

The recordings of interrogations never got a good look at the humans' faces, but he suspected the intense level of loathing was unique to him. Sure, the Captain seemed to hate all of his kind, but he seemed particularly angry at him.

Was it blame for his situation? Or something of a more personal nature?

Knox left without another word.

Clearly, Verity was a pressure point for the human—though whether it was familial or romantic, he still couldn't tell. And while he had no intention of harming her, he could imply otherwise. And there were still other ways he could use her as leverage.

OUT OF THE corner of his eyes, Knox saw Aerue approach his side. "How did I know you'd be here?"

"That was rhetorical, but since you asked, I checked all your usual places, and when that failed, I went to Verity's room."

He looked at the door, wishing he had the nerve to go inside and check on her. He'd been standing there for far too long after heading directly to her after his less than stellar conversation with her human companion. He resisted the urge to ask how she was doing. "Are you going to have another session with her today?" They hadn't done two in a single day yet, but she might talk more freely today after being thoroughly physically exhausted by her ordeal in the water yesterday. He would hate to miss an opportunity, but it conflicted with his concern for her wellbeing.

"Not yet. I wasn't sure if I should give her a break."

He raised an eyebrow. Never would he have expected him to suggest going easy on Verity. She had been right in guessing that his friend didn't like her, though he couldn't tell her the reason why without giving himself away.

"She was unusually worn out after the last one," Aerue explained, dispelling the idea of him warming up to her.

That in addition her almost drowning seemed like a very valid reason to leave her alone for the rest of the day. "Then I agree that she shouldn't be interrogated today." It was troubling to hear that a simple conversation with Aerue alone seemed to drain her more than being beaten. It made no sense. She was clearly physically strong enough to fight those who had been sent to retrieve her and to come out of her interactions with Eiz'm better off than most, and survive so long underwater. And, from what he'd witnessed, her mental strength was even greater.

Was she sick? None of the other subjects had shown any decline in health since coming aboard. And if there was a change, she should be in *better* health than the others given she'd dined with him twice, getting much better quality food than her fellow humans. Perhaps he should send one of the scientists to do another scan to be certain. Though he'd have to be incredibly explicit that only noninvasive testing was to be used. He could no longer assume they would abide by his rules under blanket statements. And even though he'd just threatened his entire population with capital punishment if they disobeyed him on this manner, he wasn't taking any more risks in leaving loopholes open.

He started walking toward the lab. Aerue followed him.

When he got there, he found one of the humans lying unconscious on an examination table with his vitals and DNA sequence displayed beside him. It said that he had increased from a mere five percent to eight after being administered two treatments.

The head scientist wasn't there, no doubt taking a lunch break, but her assistant was. "Have there been any side effects?"

"No, Your Majesty."

"Is he the only one showing improvement?"

"There are three others, Your Majesty." He was shown two other sets of data. Neither showed as steep a change as the one on the table, but they were still promising results. Then the third one popped up and it was Verity's progress. In comparison to the others, it was astounding. Perhaps feeding her Eochronian food had been a good idea. But if it was also the cause of her becoming weaker and more easily fatigued, that wasn't good. He kept his hypothesis to himself. He's share it later, after he had more time to think about it and had more information.

"And the rest?"

"No improvement yet, Your Majesty, but we've staggered the dosage in groups of three for a more comprehensive study. It will maximize the best results and minimize the most risk," the assistant added for clarification.

"And what level is the Captain at?"

"The lowest, Your Majesty. He is the second-best raw subject and we didn't think you'd want us to jeopardize him so early on in the process."

"Has he shown any improvement?"

"Not yet, Your Majesty."

"Can you safely increase his dosage again? The sooner we have more viable candidates, the better."

The assistant looked nervous and glanced toward the door, no doubt wishing for the swift return of his boss.

"I'm asking you," Knox said.

"Yes, but it is still risky, Your Majesty."

He ignored Aerue's pointed stare as he spoke. "Increase it as much as you can while still being safe. But I want him out of the lowest dosage group. If he has to be in his own level, so be it." He wanted the human out of Verity's life as soon as possible. The sooner the Captain was ready, he could get him taken care of, he would be paired up with Arfilmea which would get both of them out of his way. And, of course, it would kickstart the second phase of his program and reassure from the silent few who doubted him.

"As you wish, Your Majesty. Shall we start today?"

"If he hasn't already been given his dose, then yes." Ever since the initial scans had been completed, he had given the green light for the treatments to be slipped into the human food in the mess hall, controlled by every meal being made for each human and served to them by the guards.

Verity's food had remained untampered with, despite her being the most suspicious of the ship's provided nutrition. And it would stay that way until any issues had been worked out. Even though there hadn't been any setbacks, he knew that each subject was still unique and something could come up at any moment.

He didn't want that happening to any of them, least of all her. "I heard that our top candidate wasn't feeling well." It felt weird to not say her name now that he knew it. "Bring her in to check her health. We can't afford to have her becoming sick. And be discreet. Nothing invasive, understand?"

He stared at the research assistant until he looked away.

"Of course," he answered. "Is there anything else you needed, Your Majesty?"

Knox shook his head. "Thank you. Keep me updated."

The man bowed and did not turn away until Knox had left the lab with Aerue.

"Emotions are clouding your judgment," his friend hissed low enough for no one else to hear, but they were still in public.

"Save your comments until we are in the throne room."

Aerue shut his mouth, but he could see the disagreement burning in his dark eyes.

His friend could disagree, but Knox knew what he was doing.

The moment they reached the throne room, Aerue spoke. "You need to pull yourself together."

"Excuse me?"

"You're being reckless, and too busy insisting that you're not to see how far it's getting out of hand. As your friend and as your advisor, you need to listen to what I'm telling you. I'm not trying to control you, but this is getting serious."

"I think controlling me is exactly what you're trying to do. Or did I just take your command to 'pull myself together' wrong?"

"Perhaps I was rude in my delivery, but I stand by its message."

"You should be careful."

"If you fire me as your advisor, you're just one step closer to becoming a dictator like your ancestors."

Knox glared at his friend, but didn't answer. Aerue was right, and he certainly didn't want that to happen.

"I'll do better," he said. "But I don't want Verity harmed, and I won't budge on that."

Aerue nodded.

"Now that that's settled, I'm going to rest. Wake me up if there's an emergency."

"Very good, Your Majesty."

19

VERITY

VERITY SAW Ben's back in front of her as she was marched into the mess hall right behind him. Thankfully this time he didn't look like he was in as much pain as last time. She hoped he used the serum and didn't do something stupid like smash it in a private rebellion. It was the first time they'd arrived together and she wondered again why the schedule had changed. She hadn't been interrogated today. Instead, she'd found paper and a writing implement on her bed upon her return from breakfast. It appeared that while King Knox was duplicitous, he wasn't a liar and made good on his promises.

She'd spent the unexpected free time writing down all the ciphers she could remember from Major Davies' training. Even though she'd told Ben she knew her stuff, she wanted to make sure she hadn't mixed anything up in her memory. For this to work, her messages had to be impeccable. And short.

Ben knew she only learned the seven most popular types of ciphers, but she had finally decided on the Vigenère Cipher. It was the most complicated one she could still quickly translate. Their teacher had made them memorize the *tabula recta*, a monster of a table, so well that she could probably do it in her sleep.

She sat down and waited for the guards to set their food down and leave them alone.

When she saw his face, she knew her plan had to wait.

"What's wrong?"

"Well, I finally met your King Knox." He practically spit out the words.

She forced herself not to flinch. "He's not *my* anything. What did he do?"

"Besides order our abduction?"

She suppressed the urge to smack him and simply glared. "I meant, did he personally hurt you, you jackass."

Ben's shoulders slumped and he had the good sense to look sorry for snapping at her. "He questioned me," he answered softly, his tone tinged with confusion. Clearly, there was more he wasn't saying. If only she knew what

"Did he hurt you?" she asked again. And she'd keep repeating it until she got an answer. She'd kill him if he had. Or, at least try to. She wasn't exactly fond of the idea of "or die trying," but if she *had* to, she would. He might be the king, but no one hurt her friends and got away with it.

He shook his head. "But he looked like he wanted to punch me a few times. He kept asking about you and our relationship. He's very hung up on you. Did something happen between you two?" He didn't sound happy about the idea.

"There is nothing going on between us. But if he thinks there is, then all the better, right? Wasn't that **your** plan?" Why would he be pissed it was working? Unless he liked her too and was jealous?

Now it was his turn to glare.

Apparently not. "Anything else or can we move on to more important things?" If he wasn't going to be open with her, there was no reason for them to continue the conversation.

A muscle ticked in his jaw but he didn't say no.

"I have a way to write. I was thinking Nuit. You know how romantic Paris is supposed to be for a date. It could be like *An American in Paris*." She said the last part a bit louder in case anyone was listening in. They'd probably write their conversation off as silly romantic chit chat between lovers. She knew they weren't, but they didn't know that.

Out of the corner of her eye, she watched for any reaction, but none of the guards at the perimeter looked their way. Today, there were only twelve guards. One of them was missing.

She counted the seconds until Ben understood her hidden message. In one phrase, she'd given him the specific kind of cipher, created by an Italian woman but misattributed to a French man. Wasn't that the case over and over in history? Men getting the credit for women's pioneering work. She'd also given the key she wanted to use. Including the fact that he'd have to translate the word back into English to accurately use it.

"Are you trying to be mean?" He grumbled.

She kept her voice at the same slightly elevated level. "Don't worry. I'm not expecting you to pay for both tickets both ways. I know you'd rather save your money." She smiled and whispered, "I'm just trying to be smart about it." She lowered her voice even more. "They're already fluent in English, so it has to be complicated." It was about ten times harder than the relatively simple Caesar cipher.

"Yes, I know."

"Then stop being a baby. You've used it more recently than me, anyway. I know my dad makes you all do decoding exercises every day. This should be a cake walk for you."

"Are you sure you shouldn't pick an easier one for yourself?" He was smiling which meant he was back to his teasing self.

"Fuck off," she muttered without any heat.

He chuckled, causing one of the guards to glance over at them.

She kicked him under the table and he became serious again. "When are you thinking?"

"60?" She held up three fingers to indicate she was talking in hours. One would have been seconds, which would've been stupid. Two would have meant minutes, but was also equally unrealistic in their situation given they still had no real plan yet. That gave them two and a half days and would be during the night when she'd never seen too many guards around, despite there likely being tons of secret surveillance without them roaming the corridor. It would be their best shot but nothing was guaranteed.

"That's vague."

"It's all I've got right now," she snapped. She loved him, but he was getting on her nerves right now. "If you can figure something out faster, let me know."

"How? I don't have anything to write with."

"Then use morse code during mealtimes and hope they don't know it."

"You're not here a third of the time."

"I didn't say it was a perfect plan."

"Well, before we're hauled out of here and split up, you should know that I think I passed a hanger with escape pods if we turn left out of here."

"That's the same direction as his bedroom." The words were out before she thought better of it.

Ben's eyebrows shot up and mentally kicked herself for saying that. Now, he definitely wouldn't believe what she'd told him about nothing happening, even though it was the truth.

"Don't go there," she warned.

"I wasn't going to say anything."

"Liar. What I was thinking is that if he asks me to dinner—"

"You eat in his *bedroom*?"

She glared at him and he shut up. "If I'm having a private

dinner with him, it'll be easier for me to get there than if I had to break out of my room."

Ben cleared his throat.

"Anyway," she continued, "if you could get in there with one of the ASE scientists, we should be able to escape. I didn't see any guards keeping tabs on the area. They probably think we don't know about it."

Which made it even stranger that he would've even had the opportunity to look into a hangar. They were normally so secretive about keeping all the doors—if you could call them that—shut.

"You'd have to do it," she said. "You're a better fighter than me and have more of a relationship with the other captives. Besides, someone has to be the distraction."

He didn't seem happy with the reminder but silently nodded jerkily in agreement.

As if sensing their conversation had come to an end, all the guards stepped forward in unison and reapplied the shackles to every prisoner and led them out one by one.

She was last, and rather than taking her back to her room, she was ushered into the room where she'd woken up after practically drowning. The same woman as before stood there with another sticker in her hand.

Oh, no. She was done with their tests. Verity tried to back up but was trapped by the two guards who had brought her in. They forced her to sit down in a chair not unlike the one in interrogation and strapped her in.

The woman approached with the sticker and Verity could see that it was mostly clear, with a little blue gel at the edges.

Verity would've squirmed if that wouldn't have meant the metal restraints digging into her skin.

The woman didn't say a word as she adhered the sticker on her arm. began drawing the blood without any trouble.

It was perhaps the longest and thinnest needle Verity had ever seen, and she barely felt it go in. If she hadn't been watching, she probably wouldn't have noticed it at all.

A few seconds passed before the chamber was full and the woman withdrew the needle, discarded it, and shook the syringe to mix the fluid and testing substance.

Verity still had no idea what they were looking for, and she knew they would never tell her even if she asked. Then it turned green. What on Earth—figuratively speaking, of course since she was in freaking *space*—did that mean?

The woman laid it on a counter before spraying the puncture site with a small vial of orange liquid—probably the healing elixir again. If they weren't trying to conquer Earth, she'd bet her planet would love to know the secrets of the aliens' serum.

Verity saw her skin heal before her eyes, still fascinated by how it worked. She wasn't even sore. When she was back to normal, she glanced up at the medical technician. The woman didn't show any expression other than nodding at the guards once, leaving Verity without a clue as to whether the color was a good or bad thing. And why had they needed her blood in the first place?

The guards released her from the chair and took her back to her room.

Before the door could close her in, she said, "Can you tell the king that I'd like to have dinner with him again?"

They didn't answer aside from nodding. If they were shocked by her request, they didn't show it.

She had no doubt that he would take her up on the offer, even if it was out of character for her to seek him out. Regardless of his motives, he seemed eager to spend time with her. More than Aerue seemed to approve of, if his glaring at her during her meals with the king was anything to go by.

When she arrived, she sat down with her writing and drafted a message. It was simple: *royal dinner*, or, as anyone who read the piece of paper would see *ewehe qqtuxe* which sounded more like a fantasy dress code than a secret message.

She folded the paper and slid it under her pillow, then lay down for a nap. Who knew how long it would take for the king to reply? And if he followed his MO from last time, his answer would be in the delivery of a dress which no doubt had to be made from scratch. She highly doubted they had raided a mall before leaving Earth's atmosphere.

A part of her wished he would directly reply to her. Every invitation to dine with him had been indirect. First through Aerue and then with a dress. It was a stupid wish that she had no business wanting. Besides, he was royalty and wasn't that what they did? Delegate minor tasks to those under them? And despite his interest in her, she was ultimately still his prisoner to command. For now.

She closed her eyes and was pulled into a dreamless sleep where she stayed for a brief time before knocking woke her up. The door opened and one of the guards from earlier held a dress in his hands with shoes on top. He held them out to her and closed the door again once she'd taken the articles of clothing.

She placed the shoes on the ground and examined the outfit Knox had picked for her this time.

It was *very* different from the first one, which had been folded placed on a shelf that had been installed while she had been away at breakfast. This one was a dark red bodycon dress that seemed to transform into a red wine color every time she blinked. There was no lace anywhere to be found. Though the neckline went up to her collarbone, there was a window right over her cleavage, and there were triangular cut outs on both sides of the waist. She turned it around and cursed. She'd been wrong. The cut outs were only the front view of the entire lower back being exposed.

She couldn't help but smile. Clearly, he'd taken her advice. Though she wasn't sure if that was a good thing or a bad thing.

Aerue had passed on her suggestion about showing more skin to heart.

If he walked her back again tonight, it gave him easy access to her bare skin and she was barely able to hold herself together with a protective layer of fabric between them.

She felt the memory of his heated hand on her and shuddered. This was definitely bad, but she couldn't exactly miss out on the opportunity of learning a few more tidbits about him or his species. She wasn't going to kid herself and expect a windfall, but any new information was better than nothing.

Verity got dressed and felt the familiar compression of the snug-fitting dress. Maybe she would ask him about how they managed that. She wasn't sure if she wanted an honest answer or to see what lie he'd feed her. Or maybe he'd surprise her and be embarrassed by the question and sidestep it altogether. Though that last one was unlikely. She couldn't imagine him backing down from anything. He certainly hadn't with her.

She put on the shoes, another pair of flats, and felt something under the sole of her right foot. She took the shoe off and found a small matching band. She tested its elasticity and realized it was a hair tie.

On Earth, she practically lived with her hair up between the dancing and fighting lessons. It would be nice to finally have her hair out of her face again, though why Knox had included the detail mystified her.

Still, she wasn't going to question the small gift and quickly pulled her hair up into a messy bun. If she had a mirror, she could maybe make it more polished, but she had to make do with what she had. Why she was trying to look nice at all when nothing was forcing her besides her own vanity annoyed her but she couldn't bring herself to mess up her hair now that she finally had an option. If Ben saw her now, he'd become apoplectic.

She put her shoes on again and grabbed the folded piece of paper, slipping it into under her dress through the triangle cut-out over her left hip. Hopefully she could slip it into his room unnoticed. Even though no seams were visible from inside a room, the perspective from the outside was a different story. She'd started being able to see them and they'd only become more pronounced as time passed.

She'd stalled long enough. She knocked on the door and it opened again. She held out her hands to be cuffed in front of her and the guard didn't argue or force her hands behind her back. Maybe her good behavior was the reason or he simply didn't care. He walked in front of her like Eiz'm had, but didn't pull hard like she was recalcitrant livestock that needed to be brought to heel.

When he wasn't looking, she dropped the paper next to Ben's room and kicked it under the door. At some point during the past week, she'd started seeing the outline of doors and no longer just smooth walls, but she still couldn't figure out how they opened. The gap between the door and the floor was tiny, but the paper slid out of sight without any issues. She exhaled in relief. The guard turned around.

"I tripped," she explained, her heart racing. She really hoped these aliens couldn't hear that, otherwise she'd be in trouble. "But I caught myself."

He nodded and continued forward.

Crisis averted.

When they finally arrived in Knox's private dining room, he was already there waiting for her. She clearly wouldn't be getting another peek inside his bedroom, not that it was necessary to her escape plan. It wasn't as if she were planning on assassinating him in his sleep. She just wanted to get home and warn everyone about this species, even though admittedly that wasn't a lot.

He reached out and smoothed her cheek with his thumb. "I see the elixir worked for you."

It was such a tender gesture that she wanted to lean into it, but she straightened her spine and nodded. "Thank you." She averted her gaze, unable to withstand the kindness in his eyes. "I hate to be rude," she said, hoping to lighten the mood, "but I'm starving."

He nodded and, as expected, pulled out her chair for her. She slowly lowered herself, leaning slightly forward so he would have a full view of her back. Even once she was seated, he hesitated in pushing her in. She smiled. The dress was clearly a hit.

Then he walked to the other side of the table and settled into his own. She sucked in a breath and enjoyed the much-needed distance.

Resisting his magnetic pull only seemed to get harder every time she met him. Tonight would be a lot harder than she thought.

20

KNOX

KNOX WATCHED her surreptitiously as he poured their drinks again. He hadn't been expecting her to request a meal with him, and as pleased as he was with the development, a part of him couldn't dismiss his suspicions that she had other motives for spending more time with him.

"What are we having tonight?"

"The same as last time, if you'll forgive me. Like I said, it's a rare beast, and it would be a pity to let its meat go to waste." He'd forgone the leftovers during every meal he'd spent with Arfilmea since he last saw Verity in person. Then his chefs would have a real issue with him. And if they got too mad at him, he wouldn't put it past them giving him some food to make him sick one night to better appreciate the quality they normally served. They'd done it more than once when he was a spoiled child who didn't always like what was on the menu.

"I didn't get to ask this last time but why are we eating this if it's an endangered species? Wouldn't you want to preserve as many as you can?" She did a brief sweep of the room. "Though, I don't know where you'd keep any of them on this ship."

She was fishing for information. He filled her plate then his own and sat back down. "We brought enough of them on this ship so a few can be set aside as food on our long journey." The majority of them, however, were going to hopefully revive their species once they were introduced to Earth.

"And how long was that journey, exactly?" She cut her portion into smaller pieces using the side of her fork, frustration creating a line between her eyebrows. If he weren't convinced she'd try to stab him with a knife, he'd give her one to make the task easier. It might not kill him, but he'd still be wounded and bleeding. He'd rather avoid both.

"Much longer than you can imagine." He took a bite of food and waited for her answer.

"Try me."

He held up a finger as he finished chewing. She waited. "About four million human years."

She looked both horrified and intrigued. "How old are you?"

"In human years, I suppose I'm very old. For my kind, however, I'm a young adult."

She placed an elbow on the table and rested her chin on her hand. "You've been traveling here since Australopithecus was around?"

Technically, that was when they'd first arrived on Earth, when he was still a child, and then they'd stopped in every so often since then as they waited for evolution to converge with theirs, or get as close as possible. "You know mythology and evolution quite well. What did you study?"

"I have a strangely good memory for facts I find interesting. I haven't studied either of those topics since high school. Though I doubt you know what that is. It's also where I learned that traveling through space and entering the Earth's atmosphere caused people to age slower but also feel older."

He smiled. "For humans. As similar as we appear to your species, we don't have the same biology." Which was why they needed his program. "Our time scales are also very different."

"I'm beginning to see that." She took a sip, watching him from over the rim as she did. "I'm still working on believing it."

"You accepted my being an alien rather quickly, despite you claiming them not existing." Would she now directly admit to him that she knew about her father's work?

"I'm flexible enough to change my mind based on new evidence. What?" she added, clearly reading his silent question. "Just because my dad's job revolved around it didn't mean I thought it was an actual possibility."

"A trait surprisingly less prevalent in a species that has survived so long."

"I don't know if that's a compliment or an insult."

"Which do you want it to be?"

"Do you know that you have this infuriating habit of turning questions back around and never giving a straight answer?"

"Don't you realize you do the same?"

"I've opened up more than you." She frowned down into the cup. "Not all voluntarily, of course. Like my dad's job, for one."

"I do apologize."

She scowled at him and ate a few bites in silence. He could practically see her walls come up around her. He needed to change topics before this meal devolved into her usual antagonism towards him. "Have you been writing?"

"Yes. Thank you."

He had been right to keep Verity and the human together. Even though she was now writing secrets rather than saying them out loud, they were still things she had hoped to hide from him and his kind. "What do you write?" Would she give a partial truth or lie? He'd seen her drawing diagrams earlier today but she'd been blocking most of it as she worked.

Thankfully, Trohm had been able to fill in the gaps. It was something called a Vigenère Cipher meant to encrypt a message. Luckily, his soldier had been able to retrieve the scrap of paper after the human Captain had already translated it, giving them all the information needed to decode any future messages using the same one. They left it in the room so as not to reveal that it had been moved. Hopefully, they would continue to use the same system.

The message had a been an innocuous one but he expected future ones to be more serious than her telling him her whereabouts. Especially when the human Captain had already figured out the easy pattern of her absences being because she was eating with him or being questioned. Though, if they were planning an escape, which they undoubtedly would if they hadn't already started, her specific location was more useful than simply knowing she wasn't in the human dining hall.

"If you're trying to read my diary, forget about it."

"Your what?" It appeared she had created a third way of answering him: sidestepping the question altogether. Exactly what they'd accused each other of doing during their first meeting.

"How do you know so many things about human life and then some things trip you up?"

Because Trohm hadn't told him. And some things were unimportant. Though now he wished he knew more to better hold a conversation with her. And not just to have the upper hand by understanding all her references but to be able to fully experience and participate in whatever parts of her life she was willing to share. "Forgive me."

"So, what does it mean?"

"A personal record of one's private thoughts." Her words sounded stilted, and he wondered if she had a diary at home. He would be very interested to know what she had written.

"If you were not writing a diary, then what did you write?"

She shrugged.

He leaned back and took another sip, regarding her. There was a table between them, but perhaps she felt he was crowding her. Hopefully, she would open up more if she didn't feel cornered. "Last night, you also mentioned you danced."

That seemed to shock her, though why it did made no sense. To get to know someone, you had to remember facts about them. So, why did she assume he wouldn't recall an important detail about what she liked?

"Yes?" she said, warily. "What about it?"

"Would you teach me?" From what he knew dances allowed for close physical contact which he was starting to desperately crave with her, and hopefully she'd bee too happy dancing that she wouldn't take the opportunity to try to attack him. Though a part of him was morbidly curious about how she'd do against him in an all-out fight, it was out of the question. And he'd lose any trust he'd gained from her.

"You can't be serious."

"Why not?"

"Because I doubt dancing is why you've traveled the galaxy. And don't you have your own dances?"

They did, but there was never much passion in them. Though maybe that was him and his acute awareness that anyone who danced with him hoped he'd make them his queen. It took any potential pleasure out of the situation.

He raised an eyebrow and waited for her other excuses. She always had more than a few armed and ready at her disposal.

She crossed her arms leaned back in her chair, giving him a better view of her half-naked waist. "You'd have to narrow it down to a type of dance. And it might be one I don't have any experience in."

His hands itched to slide up and down her waist, to feel her warmth and curves against him. His cock grew hard at the image and pushed against his pants. He leaned forward and rested his elbows on the table. "Which ones do you know?"

Her eyes narrowed. "How stupid do you think I am?"

"Not at all. I think you're very intelligent."

"Then why would you ask such a stupid question?"

"Because I'm curious and I don't play games."

"Oh, don't you?" She leaned forward, her body rigid with anger and her eyes laid bare her hatred for him. "Then what would you call last night?"

He waited for her to bring up Arfilmea. When she didn't, he asked, "What about it?"

"Wining and dining me while you had my friend brutalized during interrogation."

He sighed. "It wasn't meant as a deception."

"Your intentions don't change what happened. I was getting wined and dined while my best friend was being beaten to a pulp."

"It wasn't wine."

"It's an expression," she hissed.

She was breathing hard and he could see her cheeks flushing as she grew angrier. It gave her skin a beautiful glow, not that he could tell her that. He'd likely get stabbed for giving the compliment.

"And you can forget about dancing lessons. I'd say find someone else, but then you'd only kidnap another helpless human."

"You're not helpless." Far from it, in fact.

"And don't you forget it."

How had this meal still managed to become so hostile? "I heard you weren't feeling well after you last saw Aerue. I see you're feeling better now."

Her mouth dropped open in surprise. "I am." She ate another piece of food, watching him as she chewed. He could practically see her mind working on what to say next.

"I had a blood test today."

He frowned.

"You didn't know?"

"No." Which was, technically speaking, the truth. Hadn't he

told them to perform a noninvasive in their scan to check her health. Even though they didn't use needles, it was still taking something vital from her body.

"What is it with people acting without your permission? Do monarchies work different for you than on Earth?" Her words were pointed but weren't as sharp as he was used to hearing from her. Clearly, she was more affected than she had previously let on.

"Did they hurt you?" he asked, ignoring her question. His eyes lowered to the bend in her arm. There wasn't any discoloration to reveal what happened but he could see a cluster of tiny open pores that would be invisible to the human eye if the person didn't know what to look for. He should have seen it sooner, but he'd been too caught up Verity's beautiful appearance.

"It didn't hurt," she said. "But why do you need my blood?"

He'd have to ask Dr. Mak'en what the results were. And to have a talk with her about the orders he'd given to her assistant. The man was much too respectful of commands to have corrupted the message in his relaying it, meaning it was the good doctor who had taken the decision into her own hands, and may have been the one to personally draw the sample.

"I'm sorry it happened."

She looked away from him and finished clearing her plate. He did the same, wishing he could force his people to obey him and treat Verity with the respect she deserved. They might see her as less than because she was human, but they needed to listen to their king and understand she was so much more.

He finished before her. When she was done, she lay her silverware down.

"No dessert tonight?"

"I thought we'd skip it."

He hadn't meant the words sexually as was common on Earth in what Trohm had told him were referred to as pick-up lines but he couldn't miss the flare of heat that briefly illuminated her hazel eyes. After their dinner conversation, the reaction surprised him.

She appeared to hate him and yet still want him. A human paradox he'd never before seen in any of his kind. He wondered what that felt like, to be at odds with yourself in such a way that the irrational and nonexistent divide between mind and body started to make a little sense. Sure, he was conflicted about the wiseness of wanting her as much as he did, but he wasn't against the idea—just the intensity and timing. He felt himself responding in kind and walked to the window to avoid her keen eye.

She joined him at his side and stared out at the stars around them, not close enough for them to be touching, but close enough for him to be so aware of her presence that he could practically feel her just as intimately all the same. Even in space, her blonde hair appeared like thin beams of sunlight.

He glanced down at her hands and noticed that she hadn't taken any of the utensils from the table to use as a weapon. Her dress didn't allow for anything to be concealed, only confirming that she had given up the perfect opportunity to arm herself.

Out of the corner of his eye, he saw her turn towards him. He turned his head, bringing their faces dangerously close to each other. Dangerous, because a kiss would never be enough for him. Her lips parted ever so slightly and he could see her eyes had taken on a darker amber sheen than their normal light hazel. She wanted this kiss, too.

He'd been tempted to give her one after dinner last night but that urge was nothing compared to what he was feeling now. He was probably only suffering more because he'd denied himself before. It couldn't be that he was growing more infatuated with her the more he got to know her better.

Her hands rose and rested on his lapels.

His hands instinctively reached for her waist in response. They caressed the warm, exposed skin in gentle strokes, and he enjoyed the feeling of her in hold way too much to be safe. He couldn't even rightly say he was holding her at a safe distance to save herself because he was selfish enough to take what he could but he knew even indulging his need for her in the slightest would lead to an outcome that couldn't happen. And he couldn't go there with her.

Not now, at least.

If he did, none of the protection orders he'd put in place around her would be worth anything. Even if he didn't mean to hurt or damage her, there was still a high chance rushing things with her would.

He couldn't risk hurting his plan, or worse, her. Somehow, she had become more important to him than the very reason he had taken her.

And that made her more dangerous to him than she could ever be with a physical weapon.

21

VERITY

VERITY WATCHED as Knox appeared to internally war with himself as she stroked the soft fabric beneath her fingertips.

Her hands should have been holding her fork—the only sharp object she had at her disposal—but she'd been so drawn to him by the window that she'd left her seat and followed him without any forethought. Just a need to be close to him again. Closer than the table allowed her. Which was completely ridiculous.

Her actions had nothing to do with her goal to escape, or Ben's plan for her to seduce the alien king. It was pure need and her worst fear coming true: her strange attraction was wrecking her concentration.

His hands on her waist like a welcome brand wasn't helping. He wasn't doing it in a proprietary way but in this moment she felt owned by him all the same. His palms were technically cold against her skin but she still felt heat skittering over her skin.

Verity tilted her head up and kissed him, closing the small gap he'd been keeping. His mouth was suddenly hard against hers, kissing her with such intensity that she had to grab on to his shoulders to stay standing upright.

His hands at her waist tightened and pulled her in until their bodies were pressed against each other. Her nipples hardened as the fabric shifted, then she felt his arousal near her hip and gasped. Then his tongue was tangling with hers and she felt heat forming in her belly and her skin grow more sensitive.

After what felt like an eternity but couldn't have been more than a few minutes, he broke the kiss and pushed her away.

She stared up at him and saw his eyes were once again darkened with desire. But if he felt that way, why had he ended the kiss?

"That was a mistake," he said.

The words *you're right* got stuck in her throat. It was the truth, but it still hurt to hear him say it.

She must have shown her feelings because he took a step forward. She retreated too, finally acting logically for the first time since he'd made the dessert comment. Her hormonal brain had stupidly wanted her to *be* his, but he obviously didn't agree even if his body was interested. She could relate. Didn't make being on the other end of it any better.

"I'm sorry," he said. "I shouldn't have kissed you."

She took a deep breath and stared at the floor as she said, "I shouldn't have started it."

He didn't answer as he walked past her to the door. She turned and watched him knock on it twice.

It swung open to reveal Aerue waiting on the other side. "Your Majesty?"

"Please take Miss Landau back to her room and let the chef know that he can clear the meal."

The guard took a step forward but she walked up to him, causing him to lift a surprised eyebrow, and turned around with her wrists ready to be fastened. Maybe the chains would keep her from doing something stupid again. She watched Knox with what she hoped was a cool expression as Aerue secured her bindings.

She didn't say anything to the king as she was led away. And it was the first time he hadn't said anything to her at the end of their time together.

It left an uncomfortable ache in her chest.

She didn't say anything on the walk back to her room.

"Not chatty tonight?"

She must've entered an alternate reality if he was making small talk and she was pulling his stoic routine. "No," she answered, "so you can forget about doing a late-night inter-rogation."

"I wasn't going to."

She believed him, though why not didn't make much sense. Targeting her when she was tired would make his job a lot easier, and he was passing up the opportunity. Maybe Knox had told him not to? Who knew? And, honestly, she didn't care because it meant she could go right to sleep.

They reached her door. He deposited her inside, unlatched the cuffs, and shut her inside.

Verity changed into the clean set of prison clothes. She was long past caring about the secret surveillance seeing her naked. Even if she was still hung up about it, she was too tired tonight to put much thought into it. And if, for some reason, none of the guards were allowed to see and Knox was the one watching, he clearly wasn't interested anymore. Which was honestly for the best. Screw Ben's plan. Because Knox could've asked her to undress for him in his room at the end of dinner and—the hormonal idiot that she clearly was—she probably would've done it. And it wouldn't have been as a diversion or a set up to then leave him high and dry and escape. She should be *thanking* him for putting the brakes on things and instead she was moping.

Knox had somehow successfully mindfucked her after exactly three meals together, spread over two weeks with no contact in between, and she had no idea how he'd gotten away with it. One moment they'd been arguing, and then they were at the window, and then they were kissing. It was much more drawn out and slower than the fight that had landed her on his ship, but it left her mind reeling just as much if not more.

She'd had disconnects behind her mind and body before. Normally, when learning a complicated dance routine, one normally got the hang of it sooner. Normally it was her brain overthinking it while her muscles were ready to mirror what she'd just seen demonstrated, but sometimes she couldn't get her limbs to work right no matter how well she mentally knew the right moves. Either way led her to feeling frustrated with herself until the two could align.

But this was different, and felt much worse. Because it wasn't just not getting what she wanted, but also actively making her question what she wanted in the first place. And *that* was the worst part. Because not knowing her own mind made her weak and susceptible—something she couldn't allow herself to be on this ship.

Pissed off—at herself, at him, at the situation, at everything—she threw the dress to the other side of the room, not bothering to fold it like she had the other. It hit the floor but lacked the satisfying *thunk* of something heavier.

She climbed under the blanket that had been laid over her bed while she was gone and closed her eyes to sleep. She needed to stop thinking about Knox and get back on track.

Instead, her dream brought her back to his private dining room during the kiss, replaying the memory once again as if her body wasn't still feeling his lingering touch.

But then the scene diverged from reality and instead of pushing her away, dream Knox's hands moved from their spot on her waist as one went to cup her jaw while the other grabbed her ass and lifted her against him even tighter, aligning their hips better. And then he turned them and pressed her against the window as he ground into her. She could feel the memory of him against her hip and now she was imagining it rubbing her clit through two layers of fabric with each precise movement.

She shifted under the covers to accommodate the hand drifting down between her legs. She couldn't help herself. If she couldn't get over her building sexual need for her captor, she wouldn't be able to focus like she needed to. Their kiss tonight had just irrefutably proven that so why did she want to enjoy it longer rather than quickly get it out of the way and shove it into the past where it belonged?

Heat licked up her thighs and settled in her belly. She felt her nipples tighten and wished he was sucking on them while rocking into her. No sooner had she sleepily thought it, the dream shifted to her lying down on his bed, tied up like he had insinuated on her first night, with him above working her body with his to the point of ecstasy bordering on pain. His mouth was on her breast, one hand was on her throat, and the other played with her clit as he fucked her hard and fast. She pushed a finger inside and mimicked the punishing pace dream Knox set as he plunged deep into her over and over.

And then she was coming. Both in reality and in her dream. She kept going, riding the wave until it crested again and sent another orgasm crashing down on her.

Dream Knox disappeared and she was left staring at the back of her eyelids, panting like she'd run a marathon. Her mind and body were now thoroughly worn out. She was too exhausted to feel disgusted by fantasizing about her captor, and she quickly fell into a restless sleep that kept replaying the dream intercut with memories of fighting the aliens in her room and seeing her father lying on the ground as she was forced out of her home.

VERITY WOKE with a start to her wall opening. Aerue stood there, a disapproving scowl on his face. She sat up and combed her fingers through her hair, tangling in the knots that hadn't been efficiently brushed out since her abduction. How long had she been sleeping?

"Your presence has been requested."

She swung her legs over the edge of the bed and stood up quickly. She held out her wrists to be shackled and followed him out.

Her reaction made no sense. After last night, especially after her dream compounded the issue, she should have been dreading seeing Knox again. And she *should* be thinking about seeing Ben, instead, so they could discuss escape details. But here she was, eager to reunite with him, like a lovesick puppy rejoicing when its owner returned. In a sense, he did *own* her, so maybe it wasn't that far off of a comparison. She'd already told Ben that she was kind of like a pet. All of it was fucked up.

When they arrived, Knox and Arfilmea were already eating. The future queen spared her a single glance but didn't comment on her presence, nor ask her more questions. Maybe she was bored with having a human around.

Aerue turned her toward him and unlocked her cuffs. He kept his untrusting gaze on her as he took the seat next to his sister.

Knox didn't greet her either, but they briefly made eye contact. He looked unusually tired. Had he also not slept well?

Verity mentally shook herself and looked down at the table. She could feel his eyes on her as she sat down in front of her full plate. This morning, it looked like French Toast. She hadn't eaten it in years—not since her mother died. Her father had burned it the few times he'd tried to recreate the recipe once it was just the two of them.

She used her fork to get a small piece and ate it without hesitation. She was starving. Bad dreams always resulted in her moving a lot in her sleep, so who knew how many calories she'd burned last night?

They ate in silence, and she forced herself to mentally shut out her surroundings and the three aliens in the room.

Knox might have invited her, but she wasn't going to engage

again. If he wanted to talk, he'd have to say the first word. And he didn't seem inclined to with Arfilmea in the room.

Which was strange. Because even though he'd gone pretty much mute when his betrothed had interrupted their last breakfast together, he had invited her after he already had company. If he wasn't going to acknowledge her presence, why ask for it at all?

22

KNOX

KNOX FORCED his eyes to stay on his plate. He knew Arfilmea was watching him, as was Aerue. He'd asked his friend to get Verity before Arfilmea had arrived. Having both women together again was just as uncomfortable as last time. And perhaps he shouldn't have invited her at all, given how last night had gone. He'd dreamed about her, too, which probably explained his need to see her this morning once he woke up.

But doing so had obviously been a mistake. He couldn't talk to Verity with Arfilmea there, and he couldn't talk to Arfilmea with Verity there. He couldn't even converse with Aerue about the predicament because his friend would never say *I told you so* in front of a human—especially not this one.

He was at an impasse with everyone around him, and the silence was so oppressive, it was a wonder he could still breathe at all.

Verity finished eating first—a wonder given he an Arfilmea had started before her arrival. Then again, she'd been single-mindedly eating while his betrothed had been picking at her food and he and his head guard was too busy watching the ladies to have made much progress on their meals.

Verity stood up and turned away from him to face Aerue.

He watched his guard send him a surreptitious glance before also rising to his feet and refastening her chains.

Knox glared. He couldn't exactly ask for Verity to stay longer when she had no obvious reason to.

He watched them leave and waited for Arfilmea to do the same, but she stayed the whole time he ate. Surprisingly, she didn't try to make conversation. He was tempted to ask why, but he didn't want to encourage her to break her silence either.

After his last bite, he pushed back from the table.

"What are your plans for the day?" his betrothed asked.

"Business as usual." It was an automatic reply and was normally enough to get her to give him space. But today was turning out to be against him because she also stood.

"May I join you?"

His only plan had been to seek out Verity and have a conversation with her to talk, and also learn the results of her unsanctioned blood test. Obviously, he didn't want Arfilmea privy to either of those errands. They would have to wait. If only she had asked to tag along yesterday. Then she would have seen his speech—about the safety of *all* the humans, not just the singular female—and it would have probably helped with the tension this morning.

But to refuse her would raise unwanted questions.

"Sure," he said. He headed for the door and held it open for her. They would still go to the lab to get a general update. Since his father had died and he had become king, most of his life centered around this project and now that it was fully underway, it was no surprise to anyone that he was constantly there. Although he could sense Dr. Mak'en's frustration with his regular visits.

The doctor could be annoyed, but her irritation was nothing compared to the fury he felt yesterday. The visits were no longer to merely satisfy his curiosity but also to monitor the scientists in their procedure.

When he arrived, the doctor wasn't there. Arfilmea waited by the door as he went to speak with the assistant. He hadn't asked her to, but it provided a modicum of more privacy than he had expected.

"How are the subjects?" he asked at a normal volume.

"Very well, You Majesty." The researcher's eyes drifted to Arfilmea before returning to him. "But one subject is exponentially further ahead than the others." He presented a chart of data with one number highlighted. Sixty-five percent. More than a ten-percent improvement than when she'd first arrived.

"Then why are negative side effects manifesting?"

The man cleared his throat. "I wouldn't go as far as that, Your Majesty. The fatigue may be due to the human body's need to adapt to the accelerated rate of change. The others are transforming more gradually, so I doubt they're feeling much different than usual."

So, his suspicions were right. His food was responsible for Verity's apparent deterioration. But he was relieved to know that it wasn't actually detrimental. If anything, she would come out healthier than any human the more Eochronian DNA she had.

"Would the same happen if it were applied to the others?" He wouldn't ask the chefs to give every human the delicacies he'd offered to Verity—there wasn't enough to go around if he factored in all the humans—but perhaps he could institute the humans start drinking the same morning concoction he did. If they all tired more easily, they could also better extract information from them between meals. He couldn't see any downsides, but wanted to be sure.

"Hypothetically, yes. But if you would like to hear it, I have a possible solution, Your Majesty."

Knox nodded, encouraging him to continue.

"It might be best if we continue on our course in staggering the groups and continue titrating the dosages in case something does go wrong."

"Very well," Knox said. "I'll leave you to your work, then."

He walked back to Arfilmea.

"Done already?"

"Yes."

"What now?"

"I review footage of the interrogations and testing."

"Sounds boring. Don't you have others to do that for you?"

"I like to see everything for myself."

"If you don't mind, then, I think I'll go entertain myself. I'll see you tonight at dinner."

He didn't respond to the implied condemnation of not dining with her last night in favor of the human. Nor did he offer a confirmation. She had already drawn her conclusions and nothing he said would change her mind.

He turned away from his betrothed and walked back to his private quarters. Aerue had been right about watching recordings around his people being a bad idea. At least on his own, he could replay whatever he wanted as many times as he pleased. And it would pass the time until he could see Verity again.

If he couldn't speak to her now—she was likely being interrogated by Aerue this very moment—perhaps he could persuade her to share another meal with him, undisturbed by additional guests. He would just have to keep his distance a little bit longer until he could give in to what he couldn't last night.

In the meantime, he was going to catch up last night's surveillance recording of her.

23

VERITY

VERITY'S only thought after her interrogation was a nap. Maybe her body had finally adapted well enough to being in space that it had resumed her usual afternoon slump where she would nap in the library during a long break between classes on campus. She lived too far away for a trip home to be worth it. She'd miss the second half of her classes and that wasn't an option.

This time, she had revealed more information about the on-base security protocol—though, why Aerue needed to ask was a mystery. The alien soldiers had already effectively broken in despite the alarms eventually sounding. Were they planning another raid? Or worse, an attack?

When she reached her room, a blue dress awaited her. Which meant that she'd be having dinner again. An exciting prospect, but not because of spending more time with Knox. This time, she was determined to use it as the diversion she and Ben had agreed on. She quickly wrote out a message saying as much but much more succinctly: *escape tonight.* Encoded, it read as a seemingly meaningless string of letters: *raihir buubtpz.* She folded it and slipped the note under her pillow again before an overhead camera would be able to capture its contents. One message was likely impossible for someone else to crack, but having two would make it that much easier. She just hoped the guard would make her walk behind him, or there'd be no shot of pulling it off.

This one was much more modest and covered a lot more skin than last night's, and even the one before that because the fabric was opaque and covered her collarbone, only exposing her shoulders in cut outs. Knox was clearly going out of his way to over-compensate in the opposite direction from the revealing outfit she'd worn during their last nighttime encounter.

She touched her lips, remembering the heat of their kiss.

He'd been avoiding her since then but the new invitation was the opportunity she'd been waiting for.

Examining the dress, she could see there were small sleeves that would effectively bind her upper arms but if she lifted her arms with enough force, they might break.

She'd definitely be ripping some seams as she fought her way out of Knox's chambers on her way to the hangar.

Verity lay down and closed her eyes. She had time before dinner and she'd need plenty of rest to prepare for tonight.

When she woke up, she got dressed and palmed the note in her hand, squeezing it in her palm as she held her hands out, palms down, to be shackled by the guard. It wasn't Aerue, so she wasn't as worried about getting caught.

Like last time, she kicked the note under the door and rested a hand on it to pretend to fix her shoe. Only to find herself falling into the room. Ben wasn't there, but she'd somehow finally opened a door on her own.

The guard stopped in front of her and pulled her up and out of the room, thankfully failing to notice the note she'd left behind.

He didn't say anything as they continued walking, but she was sure Knox would find out soon enough. The questions was just if he'd learn the information before she got there. She'd never seen a guard converse with a physical system but she couldn't necessarily rule out mental communication. For all she knew, they could be telepathically reporting on her this whole time. Maybe *that* was why Aerue never spoke. Because he was busy conversing with his king.

They reached Knox's suite and she was untied before ushered through, the door closing behind her. Alone again with the man who held her fate in his hands. Tonight, she'd be taking it back and getting the hell home.

24

KNOX

KNOX PACED IN HIS ROOM, waiting for the telltale sound of the guard's arrival with Verity. He hadn't been sure she'd come, but he'd seen the recording of her examining the dress and writing another note. She had something planned, but he was too desperate to see her again to rescind the invitation.

When she arrived, he was already seated. He'd precut the food and poured her drink to avoid getting any closer to her than necessary. He rose from his seat but didn't walk around the table to otherwise greet her. He would be on his best behavior and keep his distance.

She lifted a single eyebrow, but didn't say anything as she walked closer.

Her hands were empty, which meant she'd clearly delivered her message to the Captain. He pushed the concern aside and focused on enjoying the here and now. Even more covered up, she was beautiful.

She picked up her goblet and held it out to him.

He stared at it. Did she want to switch again? Hadn't she gotten over that?

"You've never heard of cheers?"

He remembered the human custom now and lifted his glass. "What are we toasting?"

She stared at him a moment, considering her next words. "Great food?"

"And good company," he added. He was glad he had when she blushed.

"And good company," she echoed, tapping his chalice with her own before taking a drink.

He did the same.

She looked down at the food then up at him. Understanding lit her eyes. She stood up and walked to the side of the table for easier access, taking the serving utensils and filled her plate.

It was no different than what he'd done every time they'd had dinner and yet having her near when it wasn't his deliberate choice was affecting him more than when it was his decision that closed the distance. He waited until she was back in her seat before he portioned out his meal.

They ate in silence but multiple times he could tell Verity was holding herself back from wanting to speak even though her mouth never actually opened. When it came time to refill her drink, he merely pushed the carafe towards her. She took it without comment.

When he'd invited her, he had fully expected her usual quick-witted sniping at him, or even her apparently genuine questions. And she'd be entirely in her right to ask him what he was thinking after he'd cut their night short last time. He'd never experienced silence from her. None of her men had either. She talked to every guard who ever escorted her from her room to him, even though none but Aerue ever responded. Eiz'm was the exception, of course, as her silence had been her only recourse when he had been interrogating her.

As silly as it was, he missed hearing her voice.

When he was done eating, he waited for her to catch up. Was it just his imagination or was she going slower than usual?

And was it deliberate or another side effect of the transformation?

He pushed the tray of dessert toward her, letting her have the first pick of the small spread. Hopefully, the extra options made up for his rudeness.

"What are these?" she asked. She pointed to a bowl of shining red spheres. "They look like marbles." She picked one up and held it up for closer inspection. "Or a really round ruby."

Neither was accurate. "I suppose you would call it candied fruit."

"What fruit?"

"It roughly translates to *daydream pomegranate*."

She put it back down. "I think I'll pass."

"It's very good."

"I'm sure." She pushed the bowl back towards him. "I know you're not very familiar with Greek mythology—"

He didn't bother correcting her mistaken assumption.

"But eating a pomegranate isn't a great idea. Apples, either, now that I think about it. Anything red in a story is normally evil in some way."

"And you think this is evil?" He popped one in his mouth.

"Maybe that's too strong a word. But hearing *daydream* as part of a food's name has other connotations."

Mind-altering. Which meant she wanted to stay alert for her plan. Unsurprising, but it made him all the more curious to know what she was up to. She hadn't gone looking for the carving knife. Her eyes hadn't even drifted much from her plate aside from when they were focused on him instead of the food.

He was tempted to tell her the fruit wasn't what she feared. It was actually named because of the way the plant grew almost on its back as if it were staring up at the sky and contemplating the mysteries of the universe. The plant wasn't sentient, of course, but anthropomorphism wasn't exclusive to humans projecting their thoughts and emotions onto inanimate objects.

He was fully aware that elsewhere in other galaxies that he hadn't yet seen might have sentient plants that neither Khavraid nor Earth did. Humans seemed less willing to accept that life existed elsewhere despite their continual search for exactly that.

"What about this one?" she asked, gesturing to the second dish.

The green squares were a pure bite of the iccubana plant. It was a bit more sour than the dessert she'd had last time. He told her so.

Curious, she held one close to her face and licked it, her tongue briefly making an appearance to taste the treat. A second passed before she grimaced.

He chuckled, which earned him a glare.

"I think I'll stick to what I know," she declared, taking a piece of the clear, sweet cake. "I hope that doesn't offend you."

"Not at all." He took two daydream pomegranates and two iccubana cubes. He'd let her have the whole cake.

She noticed. "You're not going to have any of… this? What is this called, anyway?"

"Cleatil." He didn't offer further explanation. There was no need to spoil her appetite. "And I ordered this meal for you. I'm happy you're enjoying it."

She finished her bite and swallowed. "Thank you."

He nodded. "Of course."

She was staring at him again.

He cleared his throat. "About last night—"

She blushed. "I'm sorry. It was my fault. I shouldn't have kissed you."

She was repeating what he'd said then, but he still felt the need to explain himself. Without giving her the whole truth, of course. The question was… what did he say? "It's not that I'm not attracted to you—"

Verity put down her utensil and gave him her full attention.

He kept going, "but I have responsibilities to my people." True.

"And a fiancée, who I'm sure isn't a fan of me."

He couldn't disagree.

Now, it was her turn to clear her throat. "I'm... flattered, but why are you telling me this?"

He raised an eyebrow. She was turning down the opportunity to learn more about him?

Granted, he wasn't sharing much but she had been very eager to learn about him in the past. Had his rejection made her lose interest? Or was her secret plan occupying her mind so much that she didn't have room to entertain more facts about his kind?

"I felt I owed you an explanation."

"Thank you."

She ate a few more bites, then pushed back from her seat.

This time, he walked over to her, his hand on her back as he led her to the door.

He had barely opened it when suddenly she jerked her head back, hitting him square in the nose. He took a step back.

How had he let his guard down so much?

Before he could respond, she ran out the door.

The man standing guard looked over his shoulder and after seeing his expression, took off, too.

Knox wasn't hurt at all, but he had been surprised. He followed but didn't run. She wouldn't be able to get very far. Especially once they realized she wasn't shackled. It was a dead giveaway that something had gone wrong.

Aerue would definitely ban future private meetings with her after this.

He could hear her fighting his soldiers and wished he could see around corners to know what was happening before he reached her. He picked up his pace a little, eager to see how she was faring.

25

VERITY

VERITY KICKED the guard on her left in the chest, causing him to fall back a step, hitting his head on the wall. His helmet disappeared and she was staring at Tristan.

She was still staring at him when another guard seized her hair in a fist. She grabbed his hands and turned under his arm to twist the other's wrist until he let go of her. It would've broken a human's bones, but she didn't feel or hear any crunch as she performed the move.

Once free, she grabbed the shackles off Tristan's waist and bound him in his own manacles behind his back. Thank God for the fact that Eiz'm had been an asshole and shackled her arms in front of her. Otherwise, she wouldn't have known to how to activate the stupid thing, or that there was an extra way to bind someone's feet, too.

She shoved him in front of her as a shield, forcing him to take a few blows from his fellow soldier. Served him right for betraying her and Ben by being an alien mole on their base.

She wrapped the leash's handle around her fist so her prisoner didn't get away and, still holding it, grabbed the other by both shoulders and kneed the guard in his chest. Before he could recover, she stamped on his knee cap in as hard as possible until he buckled and fell to the floor.

She could hear Knox getting closer from behind her. Time to go. She grabbed her ticket out of there by the neck with her free hand urging him forward. Guards came out of doors on both sides and she quickly pivoted, avoiding all the hits and attacks behind her prisoner. It felt good to finally be the one holding the reins.

They kept going until Aerue stood in front of them. It was the first time she'd seen him in armor and he looked much more intimidating in it than his usual uniform. He didn't immediately attack, but she wasn't going to wait for him to go on the offensive. She dropped the leash to step on it, still thwarting Tristan's ability to escape, and aimed a left-handed punch at the head guard's throat, only to have him catch her fist in a punishing grip. She launched a right-hook at his jaw. He took the hit without flinching, his head not even moving as she made contact.

"Let her pass. We cannot lose one of our own."

"Your Majesty," Aerue objected. "I don't think that's a very good idea."

"Do what I said. And tell every soldier to stand down."

"Even the ones in the hangar?"

Had they gotten Ben, or had he cut his losses and left without her? She almost hoped it was the latter, even if it meant being stranded on the ship with Knox, who now knew of her secret plan. As long as it worked for someone, that was what mattered.

"Yes, Aerue. All of them."

He pressed a button on his armor and relayed the message.

Her skin prickled as Knox approached her, standing right behind her. She refused to turn around.

"You may go," he said.

"But release Trohm," Aerue demanded, holding out his hand.

Was that Tristan's real name? He clearly hadn't been too

creative in picking a human name. And the first two letters of both were also the same as traitor.

Now that none of the soldiers would attack her, she reached down and grabbed the leash handle. She jerked it tightly, earning a grunt from Trohm. It was good to know that the alien technology worked on them, too. Though she wasn't going to press her luck and assume that he wouldn't eventually break out of it if she gave him too much time. "I don't think so. Your king here all but confirmed that he's the reason why I'm safe from attacks. You think I'd voluntarily give that up?"

"That's not true. Verity—," Knox started.

"In all my time here, I *never* said you could use my name," she snapped. "Only friends can, and none of you fit that description. Now, step aside."

Aerue stood his ground for two seconds before turning to the side, allowing them to pass. Clearly, Knox had given him permission. She hated that her escape had turned out to not be one at all. Her progress was only because the king was letting her go, which made absolutely no sense and was something she could worry about once she was gone and on her way home.

And now Trohm would make sure of it.

She forced him forward again, and she watched for any soldiers who might launch a sneak attack. Knox had given an order, but she knew from experience that not all under his command obeyed him. They walked until they reached the hanger. There, Ben and one of the younger ASE scientists were waiting.

They were both still wearing their prisoner clothes. Apparently, they couldn't find the ones they'd been kidnapped in. She hadn't either, but because of her dinner date with Knox, she looked more like she was at a red carpet event than on the run. Then again, she'd seen spy shows and movies where the leading lady wore dresses similar to hers.

Ben quickly took in her appearance and she saw his jaw clench. Did he not like it? Or did he not like the reason for it?

"Where are the others?" she asked.

"I couldn't find any of them. And what the fuck is Tristan doing in one of their uniforms?"

"He's one of them, Sherlock. Has been all along. Probably the one who let them on base. And his real name is Trohm. Now, let's go before Knox changes his mind and has the guards imprison us again. You can ask me more questions once we're out of here."

"He's the reason they left us alone? There's no way they'd let us go that easily."

"I know, but can we worry about that once we're in space?" She shoved Trohm in front of the door. "Open it."

"It requires verification."

"I'm sure you have something more advanced than an eye scanner, so don't think you an con me into releasing your hands."

He remained silent.

Before she could hit him, Ben stepped up and did the honors, snapping his head back with the hit. "We trusted you, you asshole. And Verity might be convinced we need you, but I don't agree. Do what she says before I decide to cut our losses."

Trohm buckled, but she wasn't sure if it was out of fear or resignation. Clearly, he realized that none of his kind were going to attack them in order to rescue him.

He leaned forward and the side of the small space ship disappeared like a hologram dissolving in concentric circles, creating a hole for them to walk through. Her dad would have a field day in having the mechanics study the ship and recreate it, especially since they'd have Trohm to interrogate.

She pushed him inside and followed him in. Ben ushered the scientist in after her and then finally climbed in himself. The opening closed, sealing them inside.

"Ben, you're piloting this thing. And you—"

"Joseph," he supplied. "But you can call me Zeph."

"Joseph," she repeated. Kind of an old-man name for such a young person, she thought. "You're going to help him."

"Miss, I don't know how—"

"First of all, don't call me 'Miss,'" Eiz'm called her that and she hated it. "Second, you'll figure it out. Besides," she shoved Trohm into one of the back seats and watched straps appear to hold him in. Still holding the leash, she sat next to him in the neighboring seat. "You'll have help. Won't they?" she growled at the alien.

He didn't answer.

"That reminds me," Ben said, pulling two things out of his waistband. "I snatched one of each on our way out."

She looked closer and saw a needle and a syringe with clear liquid. "Is that—?"

He nodded. "I thought your dad and ASE would want some, but we could probably spare a drop or two, right?"

She took it from him and took off the cap. Before Trohm could protest, she stuck him in his deltoid muscle, right where a flu shot would go, and lightly pressed the plunger until she saw it move a hair. She pulled the needle out, detached it from the barrel and handed it back to Ben. He stowed it in his waistband again.

Now that it wasn't being used on her, she'd never been happier that this formula existed.

They took their seats as her safety belts formed in an X-shape, pulling her back into the seat back.

"I don't even know where to start," Ben said, looking at the controls. "What about you?" he asked Joseph.

From what she could see, there weren't buttons like she had seen in every flying machine ever but instead had a small hole and large one where things were clearly supposed to go. They didn't look that different from alien space ships shown in comic book films, though she doubted any of them knew how close they'd gotten. It's not like it would make sense for there to be an alien mole in Hollywood but that didn't mean there wasn't.

She yanked on the chain, prompting Trohm the same way Eiz'm had during her interrogation. "You need a key and a destination orb."

"From the head of the army with permission from the king."

"Fuck."

Verity glanced at the scientist. He couldn't be older than thirty but she hadn't expected that to come from him. He seemed too academic to curse, though she bet even the the most censored person on Earth would let a few fly if they were in the same situation.

Would Knox really let them get this far only to thwart them now? "Search everywhere. Something has to be here." She leaned forward and the straps didn't move. She glanced at Trohm. "How do I get out of these?"

"Tap the center twice."

She did and started walking around the compartment. Ben and the scientist were searching the front so she worked on the back, looking behind all the seats and under them.

She shoved Trohm's legs out of the way and reached under, searching for anything. Her hand closed around something smooth and round.

She pulled it out and saw that it was small enough to fit into one of the holes. "I have one!"

A few moments later, Joseph lifted his hand holding a larger orb.

She handed hers to him and he handed both to Ben.

They all took their seats again. "Now what?" she asked Trohm.

"You plug them in and program each one individually."

"How?"

"You tap it until it glows and then you enter coordinates."

"I don't know stellar coordinates," Ben retorted.

"I'm a junior scientist at ASE so I can probably help with that," Joseph said, "but we probably don't have anything precise enough to land us at a specific destination on Earth. There's also a chance that we could get stuck in its orbit and never land."

"That's okay, Joseph," she said.

He looked over his shoulder. "You can call me Zeph."

She nodded. "Just do the best you can. Trohm?" She yanked his chain. "A little help, please?"

She drew out the last word and injecting an excess of saccharinity to annoy him. He'd always hated when she asked in that tone to hang out with him and Ben when she was younger.

"Area 51 should already be one of the saved options. You don't have to worry about getting trapped in the atmosphere or locking orbits. Our systems account for that and compensate."

Just show many times had these aliens secretly been to Earth without anyone knowing? Were Tristan's vacations home actually trips to space to report on them? Probably, now that she thought about it. The moment they were back on Earth, she was going to beat the shit out of him. And then she'd let Ben have a turn. And her father would probably want one, too. And that wasn't even the torture they'd likely inflict on him during interrogations.

Karma was a real bitch, and for once, she'd be helping deal it out rather than be the one taking it in the teeth.

That said, he was giving a lot of information he didn't need to. Did he have secret orders that required them to safely get back home? Probably to spy on them even more. The death penalty was no casual matter, but it might be best for them all if he were killed rather than kept alive for his intel and research purposes.

"If that's the case, then we're all set to go," she said, thinking out loud. To Trohm, she added, "You could've been more straightforward in your answers."

"The serum makes it impossible to lie and nothing more."

She knew that from experience, but still. It was a pain in the ass. She could almost sympathize with Eiz'm having to deal with her and Ben refusing to cooperate. Still didn't excuse him for being a violent, mutinous asshole.

Who was worse? Trohm, who'd betrayed her trust, or Eiz'm who had proven himself to be a physical threat who actively hurt her? But physical wounds healed. Which reminded her of something. "Did you also take the healing serum?" she asked Ben.

"Yeah. But there's not a lot left."

"Even if there are only a few milliliters, we should be able to analyze and synthesize a version from it," Joseph said.

"That's great to hear," Ben said, "but if we could focus on the task at hand. I have a feeling that we're overstaying our reprieve if we don't get out of here now."

"I can do it," Trohm said.

"Hell no," Zeph responded, the same time Ben shouted, "No fucking way."

"Do you promise not to sabotage us and set the proper course for our home on Earth?"

"Yes."

"Are you fucking insane?" Ben asked her.

"He can't lie. We can have him set our destination so we don't screw it up and then he'll be tied up again."

"You shouldn't untie him at all."

"Fine," she said.

Following the instructions on the fastener, she double tapped his straps to release him and pulled him up to the front of the pod. "Get us home."

"You put a hand over the small orb and you just scroll like you do a mouse and select the coordinates. I'll tell you which ones it is."

"Promise to give us the correct answer?"

He made a face. "I just said yes, didn't I?"

She smiled. "Just checking."

Together, they watched Zeph do as instructed.

"Stop. You passed it three up. You tap it to select it."

The scientist did.

"What about the large orb?" Ben asked.

"It's your star map. Helps you avoid getting hit by asteroids or comets or being sucked into black holes."

It was nice to know that the information Earth had about space wasn't completely wrong—aside from the glaring misconception that if there was other intelligent life in the universe that there was no way it would know about them because everything was too far away. Knox had said they'd been traveling for four million years, so Earth wasn't wrong about the distance but they were about being discoverable by other species.

And that had made them vulnerable to being infiltrated by snakes like Trohm and who knew how many others. There had to be more than just him because he had clearly reported on him and Ben and the USAF plans for an extraterrestrial encounter, but they had also grabbed ASE people directly from Cape Canaveral and the civilians could have been from anywhere. That required more intel than one person in one location.

Just another question they'd have to get answers to once they were home again.

"How?" she asked. "Is it autopilot or do we have to steer?"

"Auto," he answered.

"Great." She shoved him back in his seat and stayed standing until he was strapped in again before sitting back down herself. The last thing she needed was to be launched through the cabin when the ship took off.

"The large one also handles your speed, though I wouldn't touch that if I were you. You'd likely kill us all before we got back to Earth. It's already set for cruising speed and will get us back within a few hours."

"That fast?" Zeph asked.

Trohm didn't answer and instead of forcing him to, Verity was thinking about what he'd said. He needed to arrive alive. And it almost sounded like they all had to, which was strange. It felt like an extension of the rule that she not be harmed. Which she still didn't understand the reasoning for. Even when she was escaping, the guards hadn't actively tried to hurt her, merely detain her. "Don't want to die in space, Trohm?"

"Not particularly, no. I don't think you do, either."

"Is that it?" Ben cut in, clearly annoyed and impatient with their former friend.

"You're all set," Trohm muttered. "So if you want to get going, get going."

"Don't make me knock you out," Ben growled.

"He wouldn't have to," Verity interjected. "I'd be happy to do it while you're driving."

"I never knew you to be this ruthless," Trohm said, eyeing her as if seeing her for the first time. "I'm impressed, Verity."

"Circumstances change a person. Deal with it."

"Was it the kidnapping or special attention of my king that brought about this change?"

She saw Ben's shoulders tense in the seat in front of her. He hadn't commented on her dress, but she'd seen the tension in his face when she'd appeared. It might have been his idea for her to play to Knox's nice side, but every time she did it, the more she got the sense that he didn't approve. Which was confusing as hell.

She couldn't wait until she got home and could see her father again, assuming he was alive. Apparently he was the only man in her life who made it very clear where she stood with him. Ben had been like that, too, but now he was acting more like Knox with his caginess than like his old self.

But she'd never tell him that. Making any comparison between the two was a recipe for disaster. Even doing it in her own mind was a bad idea. She liked both of them in different ways even though she shouldn't care for either of them that way. Knox was an enemy and being with him alone so much had clearly messed with her head. And Ben would never get involved with her while her father was his superior. Maybe not even after that.

She needed to let the pipe dream go.

She stared out the window-like display at the front of the ship where the two displays generated by the spheres were superimposed over the view of space and illuminated in green and purple respectively.

Once the aliens were defeated, she could maybe worry about silly things like finding love but until she could have faith in humanity's survival, it wasn't worth thinking about. There was a whole song about it in a musical her father had taken her to in New York a while back. When she'd first heard it, she thought the leader of the rebellion was being both practical but also unnecessarily harsh to his friend, but now she totally understood why.

When it came down to it, survival trumped everything else. It wasn't exactly living in the metaphorical sense but it would be in the literal sense. And that was the best she could hope for right now.

26

KNOX

KNOX STOOD IN THE HANGAR, watching the ship take off. He heard Aerue come in before he saw him out of the corner of his eye. "You think I made a mistake."

"You let the two best candidates of your program escape. With our best spy. I don't see how any of this was wise."

"I think it's time I go down and investigate for myself."

"And leave Eiz'm in charge? Are you crazy?"

"No. I'm leaving *you* in charge."

"Who will guard you?"

"Trohm is not our only plant on Earth. Not even the only on their precious military base. This may be a setback, but we still have multiple subjects who are viable for research."

"I still think it's a mistake to go down by yourself. By the time you arrive, Verity will likely have told everyone what happened. They'll know what you look like. You will be hunted like a lowly animal."

"We both know that I have a better chance of surviving an altercation with a human than another type of their prey."

"It's a bad idea."

"You've already made your position clear."

"But there's nothing I can do to change your mind."

"Precisely."

"What about my sister?"

Knox turned toward his friend. "What about her?"

"You're leaving her."

"Temporarily. We already agreed to continue delaying the wedding until this project was resolved."

"I doubt she knew you'd be pursuing the human when you came to that decision."

Aerue had never expressed displeasure at their delayed nuptials ever before. It had to be Verity.

Knox didn't answer. "Prepare my things and a ship for me."

"Yes, Your Majesty."

If Verity thought she was through with him, she was about to be greatly disappointed.

27

VERITY

VERITY WAS busy watching out the window as they moved through space when Zeph cleared his throat in the front passenger seat.

"They might attack us."

"I can almost guarantee it," Trohm said, sounding entirely too amused for the grave danger that posed to all of them. "You are driving one of our vessels now. For all they know, it's another attack."

"I hate to agree with the traitor, but he's right," Ben chimed in.

"Is there a speaker system on this?" she asked. "Can I speak to them as we get closer?"

"You might want to start soon. We're about to pass Mars," Trohm added.

She was still blown away by how fast this thing moved, especially since she couldn't feel any motion at all. It was even smoother than when she'd ridden the Eurostar. Of course, there were faster trains in the world but none of them came even close to the rate they were currently going.

"It would help if you told me *how*," she replied. "I'm sure you don't particularly care if we die, but you might too if you don't help us."

He glanced up, and she noticed a small round indentation. It said, *touch to broadcast.*

"That's it?"

"What's what?" Ben asked. "What's going on back there?"

"I found out how to communicate with Earth so they don't try to shoot us out of the sky."

"What do you mean you *found* it?"

"It was labeled."

Zeph turned around and saw what she was pointing at. "Uh... Verity? I can't read that."

"What do you mean?" It was clear as day to her.

"It's Eochronian," Trohm explained smugly.

"What the hell?" Ben demanded. "When did that start?"

"I have no idea!" she replied. But probably around the time she'd fallen into his room earlier that night. She assumed no human could open any of the doors on the ship, but she could.

Before she could grill Trohm any more, he said, "If you're going to declare yourself, you should start now. It looks like a few satellites are being rotated towards us."

"If this is a trap, I'm making sure you die along with us," she said before hitting the button. "Hello. My name is Verity Landau. I'm a human from Earth. My father is Major General Landau of the United States Air Force. Please do not shoot us down. I repeat: please do not attack."

"How will we know that worked?" Zeph asked.

"See for yourself," Trohm answered.

Verity leaned forward, and sure enough, the scanner that had lit up in red indicating hostile powers slowly turned each dot green. What a convenient piece of technology.

They finally arrived outside the base. She didn't want to risk landing within the walls in case they were still attacked.

She pushed Trohm out first and saw her father standing at the front of the military personnel gathered in anticipation of their arrival.

She handed the traitor off to Ben and ran to her father, hugging him close.

Verity pulled back when she felt his tears on her shoulder, and looked him in the eye. "I'm okay, Dad."

"I thought I'd lost you."

"I thought you were dead."

He cracked a watery smile. "I got better."

"I have so much to tell you," she said. "But first," she motioned Ben and Zeph forward with Trohm. "Tristan is one of them. And his name is really Trohm."

Her father's features became stone as he absorbed her information. He called out a name and a soldier stepped forward to take Trohm from Ben.

"If you want to interrogate him, they have a really powerful truth serum."

Ben handed over the syringe. "We don't know what the dose is, but they only needed to use a few drops on us."

She cast her eyes down, remembering all that she'd shared with her captors.

"I'll need to officially debrief both of you, but for now, go home and get changed."

"Yes, Sir," Ben said and walked off.

"Who is this?" Her father asked.

"That's Joseph. He works at ASE."

"Do you need an escort back to Langley?"

Zeph glanced at her before meeting her father's gaze. "No, Sir. I think I might be more helpful here given I was also a captive."

"Then we'll find you somewhere to stay."

Another soldier stepped forward. "Follow me."

Verity watched as he walked away, too.

"Let's get you home," her father said.

Verity went up to her room and climbed into the shower,

leaving her discarded dress in a bag at her door. It was evidence, though she doubted there was much to glean from it.

When she walked out with a towel in her hair and another around her, she came up short.

A piece of paper lay on her pillow. She grabbed and paled. It was her last note to Ben where she'd announced their escape.

She flipped it over and saw in a neat scrawl: *See you soon.*

She shivered and dropped the note.

Fuck.

———

End of Book 1

ALIEN PRONUNCIATION GUIDE

Eochron - ee-yo-kron
Eochronian - ee-yo-crone-ian

Aerue - aye-rue
Arfilmea - ar-fil-me-ah
Eiz'm - eyes-um
Knox - nox
Trohm - tro-m
Quallokh - kwal-lock
Zrelhlm - zrell-lem

AUTHOR'S NOTE

Important note: authors live on reviews. And so, I ask you, my wonderful reader, to leave a review on your favorite retailer, and recommend this book to your friends.

ACKNOWLEDGMENTS

As always, thank you so much to my readers. I couldn't do this without you.

I also want to give a special shoutout to my *viewers*. This was the first story I talked about on my YouTube channel and the excitement I got from my subscribers really helped me stay motivated as I worked on it in the crazy quarantine and lockdown periods of 2020.

I'd like to thank my cover designer, Alivia Anders of White Rabbit Book Design for the gorgeous cover. I cannot tell you how many people have complimented it.

Thank you to all my early readers who helped make this story the best it could be: Kelli, Kristina, Hananya, Relianna, and Dasha.

I want to send a special thanks to Natalie for your military experience and willingness for me to run ideas by you in a running text message conversation.

ABOUT THE AUTHOR

Zara Hoffman is a graduate student in the NYU Masters in Publishing Program and has been writing since she was eight years old. She spends most of her time doing homework and writing new stories because if she didn't, her head would likely explode. Her books are for young adults or the young at heart. After all, growing up is overrated.

www.zarahoffman.com
zarahoffman@zarahoffman.com

ALSO BY ZARA HOFFMAN

The Belgrave Legacy

The Belgrave Legacy

Unmoored

Taming the Alpha

Stellar Blood

Bitter Blood